Shielded By The Staff Sergeant

The Brotherhood, Volume 3

Mia Caldwell and Mylia Ashton

Published by Mia Caldwell, 2024.

Blurb

Her safety is his mission. Her love is his salvation

VIPER CONLEY, A BATTLE-hardened ex-soldier, is shocked when Sage Collins, the daughter of his old friend, appears at his door, bruised and desperate. She's on the run from a dangerous gang after witnessing a murder and has nowhere else to turn.

Seeking refuge at Cooper's remote Texas ranch, Viper and Sage grow closer, their bond strengthening amidst the chaos. With the help of the brotherhood, they fortify their defenses against the relentless threats from the gang. As Viper and Sage face these dangers together, their feelings for each other deepen, forcing Viper to confront his own fears and demons. In a world filled with danger, can they find their chance at a happy ending?

This is an age gap BWWM romantic suspense with a lot of love, a bit of action, and a pinch of spice.

Prologue—Sage

SAGE LEANED AGAINST the cool brick wall of the alley behind "Club Neon," relishing the brief respite from the pounding music and oppressive heat inside. Beside her, Chloe fanned herself with a folded napkin, her glittery makeup shimmering in the dim light.

"Girl, I swear that new DJ is trying to kill us all," said Chloe, rolling her eyes. "My feet are about to fall off from all that bass."

She laughed, adjusting the strap of her crop top that bore the emblem of the club. It, along with a pair of hot pants and a four-inch long apron, comprised the waitress "uniform." "At least you get to take breaks between sets. I've been running non-stop since we opened."

"True." Chloe nudged Sage's shoulder playfully. "But you're making bank tonight, right? Those bachelor parties always tip well."

"Can't complain," she said, thinking of the wad of cash stuffed in her apron pocket. "Though I could do without the wandering hands."

Chloe's expression darkened. "Anyone I need to have a talk with? You know I've got your back."

"Nah, I handled it. Just the usual drunk idiots, who think a waitress is fair game. Nothing I can't handle."

"That's my girl." Chloe beamed proudly. "We gotta look out for each other in this place."

She nodded, grateful as always for Chloe's fierce loyalty. They'd bonded quickly after Sage started working at the club, united by their shared experiences as young black women in an often-predatory industry. Chloe had taken Sage under her wing, showing her the ropes and watching out for her like a protective older sister.

She glanced at her watch and sighed. "We should probably head back in. My break's almost over."

Chloe groaned dramatically. "Five more minutes? I'm not ready to squeeze back into that sweaty crowd yet."

"You go ahead." Sage laughed. "I just need to check my messages really quickly. I'll be right behind you."

"Suit yourself." Chloe pushed off the wall, stretching languidly. "Don't be too long though. I need my wing-woman to fend off the creepers."

"Yes, ma'am." She mock-saluted and watched fondly as Chloe sauntered back toward the pulsing neon of the club's rear entrance, her sequined costume catching the light.

Alone in the alley, Sage leaned back against the rough brick and closed her eyes, savoring the relative quiet. The muffled thump of the bass was still audible, but out here she could actually hear herself think.

She was about to head inside when a sudden commotion from farther down the alley caught her attention. Harsh voices echoed off the walls, followed by the unmistakable sounds of a scuffle.

Sage hesitated, torn between investigating and minding her own business, but when she heard a pained cry, her conscience won out. She crept cautiously toward the source of the noise, staying close to the shadows.

As she rounded a dumpster, the scene came into view. Two men were locked in a brutal struggle, trading vicious blows. One was a stranger—tall and well-dressed despite the violence. The other...

Sage's breath caught as she recognized Mitch Ramos, a regular at the club, with a nasty reputation. His shaved head gleamed with sweat as he grappled with the stranger, tattoos rippling across his muscled arms.

Before Sage could react, Mitch slammed the other man against the wall. There was a sickening crack as the stranger's head connected with the bricks. He slumped, dazed, as Mitch stepped back. In one fluid motion, Mitch reached behind his back and pulled out a gun.

Sage's eyes widened in horror. She opened her mouth to shout a warning, but it was too late. The gunshot was deafening in the confined space of the alley. The stranger's body jerked once before crumpling to the ground in a graceless heap. She couldn't stifle her gasp of shock. The tiny sound seemed to echo like thunder in the sudden silence.

Mitch's head whipped around, his cold gaze locking onto Sage with predatory focus.

For a heartbeat that seemed to stretch into eternity, they stared at each other. Her pulse roared in her ears as adrenaline flooded her system.

Then Mitch's lips curled into a cruel smile, and Sage knew with bone-deep certainty that she was in very, very deep trouble.

Chapter 1—Viper

SOMEONE WAS PRACTICALLY leaning on his doorbell, making him extra surly as he got out of his recliner to confront the asshole. "I'm coming," he shouted, making no effort to modulate his tone.

Viper's brow furrowed as he opened the door, revealing a face from his past. Sage Collins stood on his doorstep, her curly purple hair disheveled, and her warm brown skin marred by an ugly bruise on her cheek, and a jagged cut on her arm. Her almond-shaped eyes, usually sparkling with mischief, were filled with fear and desperation.

"Vance, please, I need your help." Sage's voice trembled as she spoke, her hands fidgeting with the hem of her crop top.

He stepped aside, allowing her to enter his small, sparsely furnished apartment. As she brushed past him, Viper caught a whiff of her perfume mingled with the metallic scent of blood. Closing the door behind her, he turned to face Sage, studying her intently. "What happened, Sage? Who did this to you?" he asked, his voice low and controlled despite the anger simmering beneath the surface at seeing the marks on her.

She took a shaky breath, her eyes darting around the room as if searching for hidden threats. "It's a regular at the club. Mitch. He's part of a gang, and I saw them...I saw them kill someone at the club where I work."

Viper's jaw clenched at the mention of the club. Seeing her crop top advertising the place, his mind immediately jumping to conclusions. "You're stripping now?" he asked, his tone harsher than he intended.

She flinched at his words, her eyes flashing with hurt and defiance. "I do what I have to do to survive, Vance. Not all of us have the luxury of a military pension."

He held up his hands in a placating gesture, realizing his mistake. "I'm sorry. That was out of line. Tell me what happened with Mitch."

She wrapped her arms around herself, digging her fingers into the soft flesh of her upper arms. "I was on a break when I saw them in the alley. Mitch was beating this guy, and then...he shot him, and his crew appeared out of the shadows. I tried to run, but Mitch caught me. He was about to kill me too when I stepped on his foot with these ridiculous heels and got away." She looked down at six-inch platform stilettos. "I'll never complain about them making my feet hurt again."

Viper stepped closer to Sage, reaching out to gently tilt up her chin, examining the bruise on her cheek. Her skin was soft and warm beneath his calloused fingers, and he felt a tug of attraction that he quickly pushed aside. "You did the right thing coming here. I'll keep you safe. I promise."

She looked up at him, her dark eyes searching his face for reassurance. "I didn't know where else to go. My dad always said you were the one person he could count on, no matter what."

The mention of Rahim sent a pang of guilt through Viper's chest. He had made a promise to his old friend to watch over Sage if anything ever happened to him, but after Rahim's death and his injuries in Afghanistan, Viper had retreated into his own world of pain and isolation, losing touch with the young woman when she apparently needed him most.

"I'm here for you now, Sage. I won't let anything happen to you," he said, his voice firm with conviction.

Sage nodded, a flicker of hope igniting in her eyes. "Thank you, Vance. I knew I could count on you."

He led her to the small, worn couch in his living room, gesturing for her to sit. "Tell me everything you remember about what happened at the club. Every detail could be important."

As Sage recounted the events of the night, he listened intently, his mind already formulating a plan to keep her safe and bring Mitch and his gang to justice. It wouldn't be easy, but he owed it to Rahim to protect his daughter, no matter the cost.

When she finished her story, he leaned forward, resting his elbows on his knees. "Okay, here's what we're going to do. You're going to stay here with me until we figure this out. We need to be careful. Mitch and his crew are dangerous, and they'll be looking for you."

She bit her lower lip, her brow contracting with worry. "I don't want to put you in danger. Maybe I should just go to the cops and tell them what I saw."

He shook his head, his expression serious. "No, it's too risky. If Mitch has enough money, he probably has contacts in the police department. You show up to the precinct, and he might be waiting for you when you leave. Trust me, Sage. I know how to handle this."

She hesitated for a moment before nodding, her shoulders sagging with exhaustion and relief. "Okay. I trust you."

He stood up, offering her his hand. "Come on, let's get you settled in. You can take my bed, and I'll sleep on the couch."

She took his hand, allowing him to pull her to her feet. As she stood, her crop top rode up, exposing a wider sliver of her toned midriff. Viper's gaze lingered for a moment before he quickly looked away, mentally chastising himself for his inappropriate thoughts.

He led her to his small bedroom, pulling back the covers on his unmade bed. "It's not much, but it's clean. There are extra blankets in the closet if you get cold."

Sage sat down on the edge of the bed, running her fingers over the soft cotton sheets. "Thank you."

He nodded, his throat suddenly tight with emotion. "Get some rest. We'll talk more in the morning."

As he turned to leave, she called out to him, her voice soft and vulnerable. "Vance? Could you...could you stay with me for a little while? Just until I fall asleep?"

He hesitated, his heart pounding. The thought of lying next to Sage, holding her in his arms, was both tempting and terrifying, but he couldn't deny her request when she looked at him with those big, pleading eyes.

"Sure, Sage. I'll stay."

Viper climbed into bed beside her, careful to maintain a respectful distance between their bodies. She curled up on her side, facing him, her purple hair fanning out across the pillow.

Sage's breathing gradually slowed, relaxing into the mattress. He watched her sleep, his heart aching with protectiveness and longing. He couldn't let himself get too close when her life was in danger and his own demons still haunted him, but for now, in the quiet stillness of the night, he allowed himself to imagine a different life, one where he could explore this unexpected attraction that had developed after not seeing her for almost six years at Rahim's funeral, just weeks before his ill-fated last deployment to Afghanistan.

MORNING CAME TOO SOON, the sunlight filtering through the thin curtains and rousing Viper from his restless sleep. Once she'd fallen asleep, he'd forced himself up and had spent the night on the couch, his mind churning with plans and possibilities. He needed to act fast if he was going to keep Sage safe and make Mitch back off.

The sound of movement from the bedroom caught his attention, and he sat up, running a hand through his short, dark blond hair. A moment later, Sage emerged, wearing one of his old T-shirts that hung loosely on her curvy frame. The sight of her in his clothes sent a jolt of possessiveness through him, and he quickly pushed aside the feeling. "Morning," he said, his voice rough with sleep. "How did you sleep?"

She shrugged, her eyes still shadowed with worry. "Not great, but better than I have in a while. Thanks for letting me stay here."

He nodded, standing up and stretching his muscular arms above his head. "Of course. I meant what I said, Sage. I'll do whatever it takes to keep you safe."

She smiled, a hint of her old spark returning to her eyes. "I know you will. You always were my hero when I was a kid. I mean, aside from Dad."

Warmth spread through his chest at her words, but he quickly tamped it down. He couldn't afford to let his emotions cloud his judgment when Sage's life was on the line.

"I'm no hero, Sage. Just a man trying to do the right thing," he said, his voice gruff.

She stepped closer to him, reaching out to touch his arm. "You are to me, Vance. You always have been."

He looked down at her, searching her face. For a moment, he allowed himself to imagine what it would be like to pull her into his arms, to feel her soft curves pressed against his hard body, but he couldn't let himself go there—not now, not ever.

Clearing his throat, he stepped back, putting some distance between them. "We need to come up with a plan. Mitch and his crew won't stop looking for you, and we need to be ready when they come."

Sage nodded, her expression sobering. "What do you have in mind?"

He ran a hand over his stubbled jaw, his mind already racing with possibilities. "First, we need to get you somewhere safe, somewhere they won't think to look. I have a friend who owns a ranch in Texas. It's remote, off the grid. We can lay low there until we figure out our next move."

She bit her lower lip, her brow furrowing with worry. "What about you? Won't they come after you too?"

He shook his head, his expression grim. "Let them try. I've dealt with worse than Mitch and his crew. Besides, I'm planning on calling on my brothers."

Sage's eyes widened in surprise at Viper's mention of brothers. "Brothers? I thought you didn't have any family left?"

He shook his head, his expression somber. "Not blood brothers. Brothers in arms." He gestured for her to sit beside him on the couch. "Let me explain."

Sage settled next to him, tucking her bare feet beneath her as she listened intently.

"You remember your dad, Rahim, was my drill sergeant back in basic?" At Sage's nod, Viper continued. "He took a special interest in a few of us—me, Cooper, Sawyer, and Mike. We were a tight-knit group, the best of the best. Rahim saw our potential and pushed us harder than anyone else."

Grimacing, he recalled those grueling days of training. "Your dad was tougher on us than a damn drill instructor had any right to be, but it made us strong and forged an unbreakable bond between us. Truthfully, mutual hatred for Rahim started the bond." He smiled. "We got over that."

She reached out, brushing her fingers against Viper's scarred cheek. "He always said you were the most focused of his soldiers."

A ghost of a smile tugged at Viper's lips. "Yeah, well, that determination paid off when we were deployed to Afghanistan. Our unit was tasked with some of the most dangerous missions, the ones no one else could handle. We were good at our jobs, too good maybe. Until that fateful day when everything went to hell."

She frowned. "What happened?"

"An IED tore through our convoy. The blast ripped through our vehicles, shredding metal and flesh alike. We were all injured, some worse than others. Some died."

His hand drifted up to touch the leather eye patch covering his ruined eye socket. "I took some shrapnel to the face and lost my eye. Cooper lost his leg. Sawyer and Mike sustained serious injuries too."

She reached out, taking his calloused hand in hers and offering silent comfort. He squeezed her hand, drawing strength from her touch. "After that, we were discharged, sent home to recover and put our lives back together, but we couldn't just walk away after everything we'd been through together." His voice softened. "I'm sorry I didn't check on you. I was too caught up in my own pain."

She nodded, blinking. "I figured it was something like that." She was clearly trying to sound unconcerned, but he saw the pain underneath.

He just didn't know how to assuage it. Instead, he returned to telling her about the brotherhood. "We made a pact, the four of us. We would always have each other's backs, no matter what. A brotherhood forged in blood and sacrifice, stronger than any family ties."

Sage nodded with understanding. "That's why you said you were calling on your brothers to help me."

"Exactly." His voice was firm with conviction. "Cooper has a ranch out in Texas, far from prying eyes. So does Sawyer by now. I'm sure he's closed on his place. We'll be safe there while we figure out our next move against Mitch and his crew."

He leaned forward, his face mere inches from Sage's. "I won't let anything happen to you, Sage. I made a promise to your dad, and I intend to keep it." Viper noticed Sage's breath catch. He saw the recognition in her eyes, the understanding that he was the man her father had always described—a warrior, a protector, and a man of loyalty.

"Thank you, Vance," she whispered, her voice thick with emotion. "I know you'll keep me safe."

He nodded. "You can count on it. We leave in ten minutes."

Chapter 2—Sage

THE HOTEL ROOM WHERE they stopped after driving all day was modest but clean, providing a safe haven. Her heart pounded as Viper closed the door behind them, the lock clicking into place. She tried to steady her breathing, reminding herself they were out of immediate danger.

Yet her nerves refused to settle, a different kind of tension gripping her now. Viper's intense blue gaze met hers, his eye patch and scarred face hardening his features into an almost intimidating visage, but she knew the man beneath—strong, protective, and utterly loyal.

"Let me take a look at those injuries." Viper's deep voice rumbled, startling her from her reverie.

Sage nodded mutely, sinking onto the edge of the bed as he retrieved the first-aid kit. Her cheeks flushed as he knelt before her, so close she could smell his masculine scent. Unbidden thoughts of their shared past drifted through her mind.

She remembered a younger Viper, his handsome face unscarred, fresh out of training under her father's tutelage. Even then, his dedication and bravery set him apart. Rahim had the highest praises for the soldier, speaking so fondly of Viper that Sage admired him too through the eyes of a first a child, and later, a lovestruck teenager.

Pushing aside those memories, she focused on the present. Viper's calloused fingers brushed her arm as he inspected the jagged cut, sending sparks of electricity through her veins. Sage bit her lip, suppressing a shiver at his featherlight touch.

"Should have done this last night, or before we left," he said gruffly. "Sorry."

She shrugged. "I wasn't thinking about it too much then, but my arm does hurt now." She hoped it was going to turn into an infection.

"This might sting," he warned gruffly before dabbing the wound with an antiseptic wipe and loosening the crust of dried blood on it.

She hissed through clenched teeth, more from the tingling awareness of his proximity than any pain. As he worked, wrapping her arm in a clean bandage, she studied the sharp angles of his face. Despite the ravages of war that marked his features, there was an innate handsomeness to Viper that made her heart flutter.

Get a grip, she chided herself. He was her father's closest friend, her protector, and at least fifteen years older than her—utterly off-limits. Entertaining any romantic notions would be foolish.

Yet when Viper's intense stare met hers again, her resolve weakened. "Your cheek is really bruised now," he murmured, lifting a gentle hand to graze her injured skin.

She nodded. "It was one of the reasons I stayed in your truck while you rented the room. I didn't want anyone thinking you were smacking me around." She winked.

He frowned. "I don't want anyone thinking that either. Would you like some ice for it?"

Sage's breath caught in her throat as his thumb traced the curve of her cheekbone. She was painfully aware of every point where their bodies made contact—his knee brushing her calf, the heat of his palm cradling her face. Unconsciously, she leaned into his touch, drawn like a moth to a flame she knew could consume her. "No ice."

He seemed to realize the intimacy of the moment just then. He cleared his throat, pulling away his hand as if burned. "You should get some rest," he said abruptly, rising to his feet. "We have a long drive ahead tomorrow."

Sage could only nod, equal parts relieved and disappointed by the loss of his touch. As Viper retreated to the bathroom, she flopped back on the bed, staring at the ceiling.

What was she doing? These forbidden longings could jeopardize everything. Squeezing her eyes shut, Sage vowed to lock away the burgeoning feelings before they could take root. She would be strong, for both their sakes.

Yet as exhaustion finally claimed her, the memory of Viper's calloused fingers ghosting over her skin replayed in her mind.

THE NIGHTMARE GRIPPED Sage with icy tendrils, replaying the horrific moment when Mitch attacked her in vivid detail, embellishing what had happened to make it even more terrifying. She tossed restlessly, trapped in the memory of his meaty hands closing around her throat, cutting off her airway. She gasped for breath, clawing at invisible assailants as the terror consumed her.

A firm grip on her shoulders jolted her awake. Sage's eyes flew open, pulse thundering as she stared into Viper's concerned gaze. His eye patch and scarred features swam into focus, reminding her they were in the safety of the hotel room.

"Easy. It's just a nightmare." His deep voice was soothing, the rumble instantly recognizable. "You're safe now."

She nodded shakily, struggling to calm her ragged breaths. His calloused palm cradled her cheek, thumb brushing away the damp streaks of tears she hadn't realized were falling. She leaned into his touch, grounding herself in his solid presence.

"Want to talk about it?" he asked.

Swallowing hard, she shook her head. The images were still too raw, the phantom sensation of Mitch's hands on her skin making her shudder. Thankfully, he'd not done that in real life, but it felt all too real after experiencing it in the dream. Without a word, Viper seemed to understand. He shifted closer on the bed, wrapping his muscular arms around her in a protective embrace.

She melted against his chest, inhaling the comforting scent of sandalwood that clung to him. Her racing heart gradually slowed to match the steady cadence of his breathing. With her ear pressed against his chest, she could hear the reassuring thump of his heartbeat—a metronome of life and strength.

They stayed like that for long moments, his fingers carding soothingly through her tousled dyed curls. Sage basked in the security of his embrace, the lingering tendrils of her nightmare loosening their grip. No matter how dire the situation, Viper would keep her safe.

Yet as the terror faded, a different kind of tension blossomed between them. She was acutely aware of the hard jets of Viper's body against her softer curves, the heat emanating from him in delicious waves. An unfamiliar ache blossomed low in her belly as she drank in his masculine scent.

He seemed to sense the shift too. His fingers stilled in her hair as his gaze met hers, blue eye darkening with an unreadable emotion. Sage's breath caught in her throat as he leaned fractionally closer, the barest hint of stubble grazing her cheek.

Then his lips found hers in a searing kiss.

Sage froze for a heartbeat, shocked by the sudden onslaught of sensation, but the insistent press of Viper's mouth soon melted her surprise into molten desire. She returned the kiss with equal fervor, parting her lips to grant his questing tongue entry.

A low groan rumbled from Viper's chest as their tongues tangled in a sensual duel. His hand fisted in her hair, angling her head for deeper access as he thoroughly plundered her mouth. She clung to the hard muscles of his back, dizzy from the dizzying onslaught of passion.

When they finally broke apart, chests heaving, his eye blazed with undisguised desire. Sage knew her own features must mirror his hunger, since her body was thrumming with arousal. She ached to feel his rough hands on her bare skin, to map every scar and ridge with her fingertips.

Even as that wanton need coursed through her veins, a flicker of trepidation took root. Viper thought she was a stripper. How would he react when he learned the truth? That she was an inexperienced virgin, more familiar with hardship than intimacy? Would he be disgusted to find she fell short of his expectations?

The thought made her recoil slightly, uncertainty creeping into the corners of her mind. He seemed to sense her hesitation. His grip loosened, giving her space as confusion flickered across his rugged features.

"Sage?" His voice was a low rasp, colored with a husky edge of desire. "What's wrong, darlin'?"

She swallowed hard, gaze skittering away from the molten heat of his stare. How could she explain her insecurities without revealing too much? Viper deserved her honesty, but she feared pushing him away if he knew the full truth.

"I...I've never..." Sage trailed off, cheeks flushing hotly. She ducked her head, fingers fiddling with the hem of her shirt.

His calloused fingertips gently tilted her chin until she met his intense blue stare. There was no judgment in his expression. Only a softening of his hard edges as understanding dawned.

"You've got nothing to be ashamed of, darlin'," he murmured, the endearment rolling off his tongue like a caress. "We'll go as slowly as you need."

The tender reassurance in his deep voice eased the knot of anxiety in her chest. Of course, Viper wouldn't mock her inexperience. He was her protector. She trusted him implicitly.

Impulsively, she leaned up to brush her lips against his once more, savoring the spark of electricity that zinged between them. This time, there was no urgency, just a slow, simmering exploration of newfound intimacy.

When they parted again, he tucked a stray spiral behind her ear, his touch light. "Get some rest. We've got a long drive ahead tomorrow."

She nodded, nestling against his solid warmth as he stretched out beside her. He draped his arm over her waist, anchoring her to his side in a protective embrace. Only then did she allow her eyes to drift shut, the steady thump of his heartbeat lulling her into a peaceful slumber.

This time, no nightmares dared intrude on the protection of Viper's arms. Sage slept deeply, her subconscious mind soothed by the knowledge he would never let harm find her again.

THE FIRST RAYS OF DAWN filtered through the curtains as Sage stirred beneath the sheets, blinking slowly as she acclimated to the morning light. A contented sigh escaped her lips when she registered the solid warmth of Viper's body beside her, his muscular arm still draped possessively across her waist.

Propping herself on one elbow, she took in the sight of him—face relaxed in slumber, the hard jets of his features softened ever so slightly. Her gaze traced the jagged scar bisecting his cheek, a permanent reminder of the sacrifices he had made to keep others safe. The eyepatch was on the nightstand, and she examined the puckered scar left behind by the IED. It made her hurt on his behalf to see it.

Viper had always been her guardian angel since childhood, but last night, their relationship had shifted in a way she never could have anticipated.

Hesitantly, she reached out to ghost her fingertips over the puckered flesh of his scar. Viper didn't stir, his breaths deep and even in the cocoon of sleep. Emboldened, she traced the path of that winding mark, silently cataloging each ridge and valley seared into his chiseled features.

She had known from mutual acquaintances about the IED incident and had heard that Viper carried the marks of his military service, but feeling the raised, twisted flesh beneath her touch made it all the more visceral—a permanent memorial to the unspeakable horrors he had endured.

A lump formed in her throat as she studied him. This man had quite literally walked through fire to protect the innocent, sacrificing his own well-being without a second thought. How many times had he stared death in the face with that same stoic determination etched across his rugged features?

Tenderly, she leaned down to brush her lips against the mangled skin in a whisper of a kiss. His eyes fluttered open at the caress, his intense blue gaze finding hers instantly. For a suspended moment, they simply stared at each other—Sage's fingertips still resting against the grooved scar, her face mere inches from his.

Then he surged up to capture her mouth in a searing kiss, effectively shattering the fragile tension. She melted into his embrace with a soft moan, parting her lips to grant his insistent tongue entry. His calloused palm cradled the back of her head, holding her in place as he thoroughly plundered the velvet recesses of her mouth.

When they finally broke apart, chests heaving, Viper's eye blazed with undisguised hunger. "Morning, darlin'," he said, voice still rough with sleep and desire.

She flushed hotly under his molten stare, equal parts aroused and abashed by the naked desire simmering between them. "Good morning," she said shyly, unable to tear her gaze from his kiss-swollen lips.

He seemed to read the unspoken invitation in her heated regard. With a low growl, he rolled them over until Sage was pinned beneath his solid weight, caging her in with his powerful arms. She gasped at the sudden onslaught of sensation—the delicious friction of their bodies aligned from chest to hip, and the heady scent of sandalwood and male musk surrounding her.

"You drive me crazy, you know that?" Viper groaned against the slender column of her throat. His stubble scraped her sensitive skin in a delicious rasp as he nipped a blazing path along the curve of her shoulder with those sinful lips.

Sage could only whimper in response, arching into his questing mouth as liquid fire licked through her veins. Her nails scored down the broad expanse of his back, seeking an anchor against the relentless tide of pleasure crashing over her.

He hissed at the sting of her nails, lifting his head to pin her with a look of pure, unadulterated lust. "That's it, darlin'. Let me have every gorgeous inch of you."

His mouth claimed hers again in a punishing kiss, all teeth and tangled tongues. She surrendered to the devouring onslaught, losing herself in the heady maelstrom of sensations. When his calloused palm finally cupped her breast, rolling the taut peak between his fingers, she keened into his mouth with wanton abandon.

It was only when Viper's clever fingers drifted lower, skimming along the dip of her waist, that she managed to summon a shred of coherence. As much as she ached for his touch, they couldn't remain tangled in the sheets all day with the threat of Mitch's gang still looming over them. It wouldn't take him long to shake loose the information that she knew Vance after he found dead ends with her other acquaintances, and she doubted he'd been able to avoid using his credit card to check them in here.

"Viper...wait." She used his military moniker for the first time as she panted, reluctantly tearing her mouth from his to catch her breath.

He froze instantly, the scorching path of his hand stilling against her ribcage as he searched her face with concern. "You all right?" The rough timbre of his voice caressed her like a physical touch. "We can stop if you need to."

Sage shook her head, offering him a reassuring smile as she willed her racing heart to slow. "I'm fine, just...we should probably get going soon. As much as I'd love to spend the whole day right here..." She punctuated the statement with a meaningful glance at the rumpled sheets.

A roguish grin curved his lips as he caught her meaning. "Aren't you just tempting," he drawled, dipping his head to trail open-mouthed kisses along the swell of her breast. "But you're right—we've got a long drive ahead. Best get cleaned up and hit the road."

He rolled off her with obvious reluctance, already moving to gather his clothes. She took the opportunity to admire the flexing muscles of his back, and the defined ridges shifting beneath tanned skin with each movement.

"I'm going to shower," Viper said over his shoulder. "Unless you'd care to join me and help conserve some water?" His voice dipped into a low, gravelly timbre that made Sage's toes curl with fresh arousal.

She bit her lip, sorely tempted by the mental image his words conjured—all that toned, naked flesh glistening under the spray, water sluicing over those chiseled muscles in rivulets...

Clearing her throat, she forced her wandering thoughts back into line. As delicious as the prospect was, they needed to stay focused if they hoped to evade Mitch's gang. "I'll just take my turn after you," she said, aiming for a breezy tone despite the breathless waver in her voice.

Viper's knowing smirk told her he saw right through the flimsy pretense, but he didn't push, simply offering a casual shrug and disappearing into the bathroom without further comment.

She flopped back against the pillows with a groan, raking a hand through her tousled curls. What was she doing, torturing herself like this? Viper was a temptation she could scarcely resist, his raw masculinity and protective presence awakening a primal hunger in her she had never experienced before.

But surrendering to that simmering want would only complicate matters. Viper deserved far better than to be another casualty in her long line of poor life choices. No, she would keep things friendly between them, no matter how difficult resisting his rugged charm might prove.

The muffled sound of the shower kicking on jolted her from her reverie. Sage bit her lip, picturing the steaming rivulets cascading over Viper's powerful frame. Squeezing her eyes shut, she willed the enticing image away before it could take root.

This was neither the time nor the place to indulge in such wanton fantasies. They had a long journey ahead fraught with untold dangers if Mitch's gang caught up to them. She would need to be fully focused, alert to any potential threats.

Sage finally rolled out of bed and began gathering her belongings to get ready for their departure. She couldn't afford any more distractions, sensual or otherwise. Not until they reached the safety of their destination, or Mitch was no longer a threat.

Only then could she allow herself to fully surrender to the molten promise simmering between her and Viper. The thought made her shiver with anticipation despite her best efforts. If last night had been any indication, the conflagration between them would be cataclysmic when finally unleashed.

For now, Sage locked away those smoldering embers, steeling her resolve as the muffled sounds of the shower continued. She was in this for the long haul—and she would endure any temptation, any challenge, to ensure they made it through to the other side intact.

Chapter 3—Viper

THE WARM WATER CASCADED over his muscular frame as he stood under the shower stream, eyes closed, and jaw clenched. Unbidden thoughts of Sage flooded his mind—her luscious curves, those full lips, and the spark in her deep brown eyes. He couldn't resist the temptation any longer.

One calloused hand snaked down to grasp his growing erection as images of Sage played through his mind like an erotic film reel. He pictured her peeling off those tight hot pants, revealing toned thighs, then shimmying out of her crop top to bare her ample breasts. Viper groaned, stroking himself with firm, steady motions in time with the fantasy unfolding.

She would look up at him through thick lashes, a coy smile on those plump lips as she beckoned him closer with a crook of her finger. He'd press his body against hers, the heat and softness of her skin igniting a fire in his loins. Their mouths would crash together in a hungry, open-mouthed kiss as hands roamed freely...

A grunt escaped Viper's lips as he increased the pace, the coil of pleasure in his cock tightening and making him spasm. How he ached to bury himself in Sage's wet pussy, to hear her cry out his name in ecstasy as he pounded into her again and again...

With a guttural groan, he climaxed, hips jerking as he spilled his release against the tiled wall. He stood there panting for a few moments, the afterglow fading into a dull ache of shame and regret.

Sage was his best friend's daughter—practically a kid to him. Not to mention over fifteen years his junior. Getting involved with her would be a violation of Rahim's trust, and a line he could never uncross. He had to keep things friendly and a bit distant, no matter how badly his body craved her.

Pushing aside the thoughts, he quickly rinsed off and stepped out, grabbing a towel to dry himself. As he swiped it over his face, he heard a faint noise from the other room and froze, muscles tensing.

The door creaked open, and there stood Sage, wearing just his T-shirt. "Sorry, I thought I heard something out here," she said, eyes roving over his naked form before snapping back up to meet his gaze.

A heat rush hit his cheeks as their gazes locked, and he hoped she couldn't sense the guilt and lingering arousal rolling off him in waves. He cleared his throat. "Just me. Everything's fine." He slipped past her so she could have the shower.

He quickly dressed himself in the bedroom area of the hotel room, pulling on a fresh T-shirt and jeans with deft motions born from years of combat readiness. As he laced up his boots, a faint thud from the adjoining room made his head snap up, eyes narrowing.

Crossing the room in three long strides, he pressed his ear against the door. Muffled voices, indistinct but unmistakably male, reached him. His jaw clenched as adrenaline surged through his veins. He had a sinking feeling Mitch's gang had tracked them down.

He spun toward the bathroom, rapping sharply on the door. He didn't hear any water running and hoped he'd caught her in time. "Sage. Get dressed because we need to move now."

There was a pause, then the door cracked open, Sage's face appearing with a questioning look. Viper held a finger to his lips for silence as more noises filtered through—the sound of a door being kicked open down the hallway.

Sage's eyes widened in understanding. She disappeared back into the bathroom, emerging moments later as fully clothed as she could with no items beyond her uniform and his borrowed T-shirt, purple hair tied back in a sleek ponytail. He admired her poise under pressure as he handed her a compact 9mm pistol from his duffel bag. "You know how to use this?"

A curt nod was her only reply as she checked the weapon.

Another crash, much closer this time, made them both freeze. He grabbed his bag and ushered her toward the window, throwing it open. They were only on the second floor—an easy drop to the ground below if needed.

The door to their room exploded inward with a deafening boom, shards of wood exploding across the room as three masked men barged inside, automatic weapons raised.

"There they are. Don't let them escape."

Viper shoved Sage toward the window opening. "Go. I'll cover you."

She didn't hesitate, leaping out onto the fire escape with feline grace. Viper dropped to one knee, squeezing off a trio of shots to keep the gunmen's heads down as he backed toward the window.

One of the thugs crumpled with a scream, clutching his shattered kneecap. The other two wildly returned fire, pockmarking the walls as he hurled himself out the window after Sage. They hit the ground running, Viper grabbing Sage's hand to pull her along as bullets whined past them. He led them on a serpentine path through the deserted parking lot toward the tree line at the far end.

More shouts echoed behind them as more gang members poured out of the hotel in pursuit. Viper risked a glance over his shoulder, cursing as he saw a black SUV with tinted windows peel out after them.

"This way." He yanked Sage off the pavement, plunging into the underbrush. Branches whipped at their faces as they crashed through the foliage, putting as much distance between them and their pursuers as possible.

The roar of the SUV's engine grew louder as it left the parking lot, tires churning up dirt and leaves as it bore down on them. Viper scanned their surroundings desperately for any escape route or defensible position.

A narrow gulley appeared ahead, steep banks overgrown with brambles. Not ideal, but it would have to do. "Down there, quickly."

They scrambled down the slope, crouching low as the SUV's headlights swept back and forth, the gang members shouting taunts and threats. Viper motioned Sage further back into the shadows as he took up a firing position at the edge of the gulley.

The first gunman rounded the corner, weapon shouldered. Viper's pistol barked twice, dropping him in a boneless heap. Two more took his place, spraying the brush line violently with automatic fire as they advanced.

Dirt and rocks rained down on Viper and Sage as the bullets impacted all around them. He gritted his teeth, squeezing off measured shots to keep their enemies pinned.

A lucky shot from one of the gunmen clipped his bicep, the force of the impact spinning him halfway around. He grunted in pain but kept his weapon up and firing.

Sage pressed herself against the gulley wall, eyes wide with terror yet her hands remained steady on her pistol. When one of the gang members broke from cover to flank them, she dropped him with two precise shots to center mass.

The remaining gunman went down under Viper's withering barrage a moment later. Silence fell over the brush, broken only by the harsh sound of their breathing.

Viper reloaded with a fresh magazine, eyes scanning the tree line for any other threats. When none appeared, he turned to Sage, allowing himself a tight smile.

"Not bad for a civilian. Your old man taught you well."

Sage managed a shaky grin in return.

Shouts in the distance made them both tense again. More gang members, closing in from other directions.

"We need to keep moving," said Viper grimly. "We have to double back to get my truck, but I think we can make it. They probably left one or two guards, but they're all out here looking for us. If we stay here, it's only a matter of time before they flank us or call for reinforcements."

She nodded as she followed him deeper into the brush. They slithered and moved as stealthily as possible, slowly working their way back to his truck. She was surprised not to encounter any of Mitch's gang until they neared the parking lot. As Viper had predicted, there were two guards on his truck.

He slipped up behind the nearest one and slammed his forehead into the side of the truck bed in one smooth motion, dropping the gangster before he could even shout. As his friend turned, still trying to grasp what had happened, she hit him in the back of the head, near the brainstem, with the pistol of the 9mm Viper had given her. "I hope you have the keys," she said softly as he scooted the two fallen men closer together to get around them.

He extracted them from his pocket. "Sure do. Get in, darlin', and let's get the hell out of here."

VIPER'S TRUCK RUMBLED along the isolated Texas backroads, kicking up clouds of dust in its wake. Beside him, Sage stared out the window at the endless stretches of scrubland and ranch fences, an unreadable expression on her face.

"Not quite what you're used to in the city, huh?" Viper's deep voice broke the silence.

Sage turned to face him, tucking a stray curl of purple hair behind her ear. "It's...different, but in a good way, I think." She offered him a small smile. "Peaceful."

Viper grunted in acknowledgment, stealing a glance at her before returning his focus to the road ahead. He couldn't deny the serenity of these wide-open spaces, so unlike the urban jungle they'd just escaped, but more than that, he was struck by how out of place Sage looked here—a vibrant splash of color against the muted browns and grays.

His gaze drifted over her features, taking in those full lips, the elegant curve of her neck, and the swell of her breasts beneath the thin fabric of her new top. They'd stopped in a city with a big box store to allow her to grab a few things, so she didn't have to keep wearing just the crop top, hot pants, and/or his T-shirt—though he was going to miss her in that T-shirt. It had never looked so good as it did on her.

He swallowed hard, tearing his gaze away before she caught him staring. *Get a grip, old man. This is Rahim's little girl, for Christ's sake.*

Shoving aside the unwanted thoughts, he focused on the matter at hand. "We'll be at Cooper's place soon. He's...well, you'll see." A wry smile tugged at his lips, wondering how Sage would take the gruff, battle-hardened man waiting for them. He didn't think she'd ever met Cooper, though he'd been friends with Rahim too.

Sage was silent for a long moment, digesting his words. "I remember when I heard about the explosion from an Army buddy of my dad's, and how you'd all been injured. I wanted to find you, to check on you, but..." She sighed. "I'd just lost Dad several months before, and I was trying to survive. I didn't know if you'd even want to see me."

Viper's jaw tightened. "Of course, I would have. You're Rahim's daughter."

She seemed to flinch, as though she didn't like being reminded that was all she was supposed to be to him. He'd chosen the words deliberately to remind them both, but now he felt like crap for doing so.

They lapsed into contemplative silence. Eventually, the rutted dirt road gave way to a long, winding driveway flanked by wooden fence posts. Up ahead, the ranch house and outbuildings came into view—a ramshackle collection of structures that had clearly seen better days, but there were signs of recent construction and improvement. Having Nina and Caleb had clearly inspired Cooper to start improving his family's homestead.

Two dogs, a small Scottish terrier/mutt mix and a mastiff-mix, came bounding out from behind the barn. The little one barked furiously at the approaching truck, while the mastiff seemed to be grinning. Viper simply rolled down the window and bellowed a sharp command. "Enough, Scooter." The terrier-mix instantly quieted, and the mastiff's tail threatened to wag so hard, he might obtain flight.

Sage shot him an impressed look as he killed the engine. "I take it those are Cooper's pets?"

"Lex and Scooter," he said with a nod. "Lex is the chill dude. Scooter thinks he's badass, and he'll take out anyone's ankles, but luckily, they know me." He grinned.

He levered himself out of the truck cab, Sage following suit a moment later. The little dog regarded her warily but made no move to approach as Viper strode up to the house's weathered front door and pounded on it with his fist. The bigger dog, Lex, came bounding toward her. She seemed to be bracing herself for him to jump on her, but he stopped just shy of that and sat, wagging his tail and looking at her patiently.

She reached out and patted his head, giving him a pleased smile at the dog's instant acceptance as Viper knocked on the door. "I think he likes me."

"Sure does." He didn't bother to tell her Lex liked everyone, not wanting to steal her thunder. He pounded on the door when Cooper didn't answer fast enough. "Cooper? Nina? Open up. It's me."

There was a muffled thump from inside, followed by the sound of heavy but slightly uneven footsteps. The door swung inward to reveal a hulking, granite-jawed figure silhouetted in the dim light.

"You made good time..." The man's grizzled voice held a hint of surprised amusement as he looked Viper up and down.

Viper allowed himself a wolfish grin, clasping forearms with the other man in a warrior's embrace. "We had some trouble, but we're here."

Cooper snorted. Viper could see the moment the other man registered Sage's presence, his body stiffening imperceptibly as he raked her up and down with an assessing glare.

"This the girl you were telling me about?" His tone made it clear he wasn't impressed by her stylish appearance. He probably didn't know what to make of her, all dolled up for city life when he lived a more sedate rural lifestyle.

"That's her," he said. "Sage, this is Cooper. He'll be putting us up for a while."

Sage extended her hand politely. "It's nice to meet you, sir."

Cooper eyed her proffered hand for a beat before ignoring it completely. "Nina's awake, and Caleb's asleep, so be quiet. Get your asses inside before we draw more attention than a stripper at a prayer meeting."

With that less-than-warm welcome, he turned and thumped back into the house, leaving Viper and Sage to exchange a resigned look before following.

As he stepped over the threshold, a flood of memories assailed him—nights spent drinking beer and swapping war stories with his brothers, plotting their next move or licking their wounds, always ready for whatever fresh hell awaited them.

Those days were long gone, but somehow, despite the years and miles between them, the bonds of brotherhood remained unbroken, and if anyone could keep Sage safe until this mess was dealt with, it was the ragtag group of hardcases about to be gathered under this very roof.

Chapter 4—Sage

SAGE FOLLOWED NINA into the guest room, taking in her surroundings with curiosity and apprehension. The room was cozy yet spacious, with a large bed situated against one wall and a dresser on the opposite side. A window overlooked the vast ranch.

"Let me help you with the bed," said Nina, her voice gentle and soothing. She began smoothing out the sheets, her movements practiced and efficient.

Sage hesitated for a moment before joining her, carefully tucking in the corners of the fitted sheet. As they worked side by side, she stole glances at the other woman, struck by her natural beauty and an aura of quiet strength.

"You must have a lot of questions," said Nina, breaking the silence. "I can only imagine how overwhelming this all must be for you."

She paused, considering her words carefully. "It's been...a whirlwind, to say the least, but I'm grateful for your hospitality and for Cooper's willingness to help."

Nina nodded, her eyes filled with understanding. "We've all been through our fair share of turmoil. That's what brought us together in the first place." She took a deep breath before continuing. "A few months ago, I was trapped in a dangerous situation with my boss, Darren. He was involved in some shady business dealings, and when I stumbled upon evidence of his illegal activities, he became a threat to me and my son, Caleb.

"Darren was a powerful man with connections, and I had nowhere to turn. That's when Cooper saved me." A faint smile played on Nina's lips. "He and the others didn't hesitate to come to our aid. They protected us, fought for us, and ultimately brought Darren's empire crumbling down."

Sage's eyes widened, her respect for these men growing with each revelation. "That's incredible. I can't even begin to imagine what you went through."

She reached out, placing a reassuring hand on Sage's arm. "But you don't have to imagine it alone anymore. We're here for you, just as we were there for each other. Cooper and the others are more than just a group of friends—they're a brotherhood forged in the fires of combat and hardship."

Sage nodded, heart swelling with gratitude. She could sense the depth of the bond that these people shared, a connection that transcended mere friendship or camaraderie.

"Thank you, Nina. Knowing that you've all been through similar ordeals and come out the other side gives me hope."

Nina smiled warmly, her dark eyes shining with understanding. "You'll get through this. You're part of our family now, and we protect our own."

After making the bed with Nina's help, Sage excused herself to find Viper. She wandered through the ranch house, taking in the rustic decor and homey atmosphere until she spotted him through the window, standing guard outside.

Stepping out onto the porch, she approached him. "Vance? Do you have a moment?"

He turned, his eye scanning her briefly before nodding. "What is it, Sage?"

"The bed's all made up. If you'd like, you can share it with me tonight." Her tone was casual, giving him an easy out if he preferred to keep things professional between them.

Viper's jaw tightened almost imperceptibly before he replied. "I appreciate the offer, but I'll be on guard duty until Mike and Sawyer arrive. Can't risk letting my focus slip."

Sage inclined her head, respecting his dedication. "Of course, I understand completely. Just thought I'd extend the invitation."

A ghost of a smile played on his lips. "And I'm honored you did. Get some rest, Sage. We've got a long journey ahead."

With a nod, she retreated back inside, settling into the cozy bedroom. Despite her attempts to read and occupy her mind, thoughts of Viper kept resurfacing. The memory of his strong hands tending to her injuries, the intensity in his eye, and the rugged lines of his face—it all stirred an undeniable longing within her.

Eventually, exhaustion won out, and she drifted into a restless slumber, tossing and turning beneath the sheets. It wasn't until the first rays of dawn began filtering through the curtains that she felt the mattress dip beside her.

Viper moved with practiced silence, slipping under the covers and instinctively pulling her into his embrace. His warmth enveloped her, and the steady rhythm of his breathing lulled her into a deep, dreamless sleep unlike any she'd experienced since this ordeal began.

For the first time in days, Sage's mind was at peace, her body relaxing against Viper's as if she had found her safe haven. The world beyond the bedroom ceased to exist. There was only the profound solace of being held by someone she innately trusted with her life.

WHEN SHE FINALLY STIRRED hours later, Viper's arm was still draped protectively around her waist, his chest rising and falling with each measured breath. Sage allowed herself a fleeting indulgence, studying the contours of his face, so stoic yet undeniably handsome.

Carefully, she extricated herself from his embrace, slipping out of bed and padding across the room to grab a robe. As she cinched the tie around her waist, she stole one last glance at Viper's slumbering form, a faint smile tugging at her lips. She visited the bathroom, preparing for the day, and then made her way to the kitchen.

The aroma of freshly brewed coffee and sizzling bacon filled the air as she entered the cozy space. Her senses were immediately enveloped by the warm, inviting atmosphere.

Nina greeted her with a radiant smile, her eyes crinkling at the corners. "Good morning, Sage. I hope you slept well." She gestured toward the table, where a veritable feast was laid out. "Please, have a seat. Help yourself."

As Sage settled into one of the chairs, she marveled at the domestic scene unfolding before her. Cooper stood at the stove, his broad shoulders flexing beneath the fabric of his shirt as he tended to the pancakes. Caleb, a whirlwind of energy, darted around the kitchen, setting the table with an enthusiasm that belied his young age.

It was then that Sage noticed the others filtering in. Nina paused to introduce them to her—Sawyer, his rugged features softened by the tender way he cradled his infant daughter, Aoife. Kinsey followed closely behind, her eyes alight with adoration as she gazed upon her husband and child. Even Mike, with his brooding demeanor, seemed at ease in this familial setting.

A hush fell over the room as they all took their seats, the clink of cutlery against plates the only sound punctuating the comfortable silence. It was Sawyer who finally broke the spell, his voice a deep rumble.

"I know we're all here for different reasons, but one thing remains constant—the bond we share." He paused, his gaze sweeping over each of them in turn. "We're a family."

Sage could sense the truth in them and in the unbreakable connection that bound these people together, transcending blood ties.

It was Cooper who spoke next, his gruff exterior belying the tenderness in his eyes as he looked upon his wife and son. "When I thought I had lost everything, you all showed me the true meaning of brotherhood." His gaze flickered to Sage. "And now, we welcome a new member into our fold."

A chorus of nods and murmurs of agreement rippled through the group, and warmth bloomed in her chest. It was nice to feel like she belonged, at least for the moment. Once her crisis resolved, she'd probably lose this connection when she returned to her real life, and the thought made her lungs constrict.

Kinsey leaned forward, her expression one of genuine curiosity. "Sage, if you don't mind me asking, what brought you to us? We've all had our share of harrowing tales, but yours remains a mystery. When Cooper called, he didn't know much either."

"You came running without knowing the details. Y'all are amazing." Sage took a steadying breath, acutely aware of all eyes upon her. "It's a long story, one that begins with my father, Rahim." She paused, gathering her thoughts. A solemn silence settled over the group as Sage recounted the events that had led her to their doorstep.

Before she could begin, Viper entered the kitchen. He looked rumpled but alert as he took a seat between her and Kinsey, reaching for the pancakes after giving her a nod and a wink.

"I witnessed something I shouldn't have—a brutal gang killing in the alleyway behind my job. Before I could process what had happened, my neighbor and the gang leader, Mitch Ramos, confronted me." Her voice wavered slightly, the memories still raw and visceral. "He was going to kill me, but I somehow got away."

She put her hand on Viper's thigh as she looked at him. "I came to Viper, because he and my dad, Rahim, used to be close when Dad was still alive, and I needed a warrior." She blinked. "I didn't expect to get a whole family of warriors in the process."

As she finished her tale, the room was enveloped in stillness. It was Nina who finally broke the silence, her voice laced with a maternal warmth. "Sage, you're safe here with us. We'll protect you, just as we've protected each other time and time again." She reached across the table, giving Sage's hand a reassuring squeeze.

A chorus of affirmations rose from the others, their voices mingling in a symphony of solidarity. There was a lump in her throat, and she was overwhelmed by the depth of their acceptance and support.

For that moment, she truly understood the power of the bond they shared—a bond forged not by blood, but by the shared experiences that had shaped and tempered them. As she looked around the table, she saw not just a group of individuals, but a family united by an unbreakable resolve to face whatever challenges lay ahead, together.

And for the first time since this ordeal began, Sage felt a glimmer of hope ignite within her. With these remarkable people by her side, she knew that no matter what Mitch Ramos threw their way, they would emerge victorious, their brotherhood stronger than ever before.

Chapter 5—Viper

THAT NIGHT, VIPER ENTERED Sage's room without knocking, his gaze intense as it met hers. The air seemed charged with an undeniable tension that had been building between them.

Without a word, Viper lowered his mouth to hers, claiming her lips in a searing kiss that ignited a fire within her core. Sage melted into his embrace, her fingers clutching at the fabric of his shirt as she returned the passionate kiss with equal fervor.

Breaking the kiss, he rested his forehead against hers, his breath ragged. "Are you sure about this?"

In response, she captured his lips once more, pouring every ounce of her longing into the kiss. Her fingers found the hem of his shirt, tugging it upwards, silently urging him to remove the barrier between them.

The tension between them had been building for days, and tonight, it finally snapped. Her gaze locked onto his, and he could see the desire in them. He leaned in, capturing her lips in a gentle kiss.

Sage responded eagerly, her hands tangling in his short, neatly trimmed hair. Viper deepened the kiss, exploring her mouth with his tongue. He could feel her body trembling beneath him, reminding him she was a virgin. He would have to be gentle with her.

Breaking the kiss, he trailed his lips down her neck, nipping at her collarbone. She gasped, digging her fingers into his shoulders. He continued his descent, pulling her shirt over her head and unclasping her bra. Her breasts spilled out, and he took a moment to admire them before taking one nipple into his mouth.

Sage moaned, arching her back. He switched to the other nipple, teasing it with his tongue. She was clearly growing more and more aroused, and it was time to take things to the next level.

Sliding down her body, he hooked his fingers into the waistband of her jeans and pulled them off. Wetness glistened between on her mound, but not enough yet. He wanted to make sure she was fully satisfied.

Viper spread her legs and settled between them. He could smell her arousal, and it made him even more excited. He ran his tongue along her slit, tasting her sweetness. She cried out, her hips bucking. Viper continued to lick and suck, bringing her to the brink of orgasm.

When Sage finally came, her body shook with the force of it. He lapped up her juices, savoring the taste. His need was urgent, but he had to be gentle with her, so he could wait.

Sliding up her body, Viper positioned himself at her entrance. He could see the fear in her eyes, and he whispered reassurances to her. "I'll be gentle, I promise."

She nodded, biting her lip. Viper pushed inside her slowly, inch by inch. He could feel her tightness, and it took all his self-control not to fully thrust into her. When he was finally all the way in, he paused, giving her time to adjust.

Her eyes were squeezed shut, and he could see the pain on her face. He kissed her gently, whispering words of love and encouragement. "You're doing so well, baby. Just relax."

Slowly, she began to move her hips, and Viper matched her rhythm. Her body was relaxing, and she was clearly starting to enjoy it. He picked up the pace, thrusting deeper and harder. She moaned.

Over the next few minutes, her moans grew louder, and her body started tensing up again. He knew she was close to orgasm, and he wanted to make sure she came again before he did. He reached down between their bodies, finding her clit and rubbing it gently.

Sage cried out, her body convulsing as she came. He followed shortly after, his own orgasm washing over him like a wave. He collapsed on top of her, breathing heavily.

They lay there for a few moments, their bodies entwined. Viper could feel Sage's heartbeat slowing, and it was obvious she was falling asleep. He pulled her closer, wrapping his arms around her.

As he drifted off to sleep, he was grateful for this moment. He had never felt so connected to someone before, even the brotherhood. This bond was different. Deeper in its own way and totally consuming. He would do anything to protect Sage. He would make sure she was safe, no matter what it took.

THE NIGHT WAS STILL and peaceful when the first crash shattered the silence. Viper jolted awake, instincts honed from years of combat kicking in instantly. He was already reaching for the gun under his pillow when another deafening bang echoed through the house.

"Stay down," he said, pushing her off the bed as he rolled to the floor. Crouched in a defensive position, he scanned the room for threats.

A muffled shout came from outside the bedroom door, followed by the unmistakable sound of splintering wood. Viper tensed, tightly gripping his weapon.

The door burst open with a thunderous crash, and three masked figures poured into the room, brandishing assault rifles. Without hesitation, Viper opened fire, his shots finding their mark with lethal precision.

Two of the intruders crumpled to the ground, but the third managed to dive for cover behind the dresser. He cursed under his breath, keeping his aim trained on the dresser as he inched toward Sage's trembling form.

"You okay?" he asked in a low voice, his gaze never leaving the dresser.

Sage nodded, her eyes wide with fear. "What's happening?"

Before Viper could respond, the bedroom window exploded inward in a shower of glass. He whirled around, squeezing off a burst of gunfire at the new threat. A strangled cry told him he'd hit his mark.

The sound of approaching footsteps had Viper spinning back toward the door, just in time to see Sawyer and Mike charging in, weapons drawn.

"We've got company," he said, gesturing toward the dresser.

Sawyer nodded, taking up a position on the opposite side of the room while Mike covered the shattered window. The three men held their ground, waiting for the next move from their unseen foes.

Suddenly, a grenade sailed through the open doorway, clattering across the floor toward them. Viper's heart lurched, and he braced himself for the explosion, but the blast never came. Instead, a thick cloud of smoke began billowing from the canister, rapidly filling the room.

"Smoke grenade," shouted Sawyer, already moving toward the window. "Everyone out, now."

Viper grabbed Sage's arm, hauling her to her feet and propelling her toward the window. She clambered through the shattered opening, coughing violently as the acrid smoke stung her lungs.

He followed close behind, his eye streaming from the noxious fumes. He could barely make out the shapes of Sawyer and Mike through the haze as they retreated from the room.

Once outside, Viper took a deep, grateful breath of fresh air, his gaze sweeping the darkness for any sign of their attackers. Sage clung to his side, trembling with residual fear.

The sound of approaching engines had them all tensing, weapons at the ready. Moments later, a pair of battered pickup trucks roared into view, skidding to a halt in a spray of gravel.

The doors burst open, and a familiar figure leapt out, assault rifle in hand. "Get in, now," bellowed Cooper, his voice carrying clearly across the yard.

Viper didn't need to be told twice. He ushered Sage toward the nearest truck, covering her as she clambered into the back. Sawyer and Mike were right behind them, laying down suppressing fire as they retreated.

Once they were all aboard, the trucks peeled out, tires spitting gravel as they raced away from the besieged house. He pulled Sage close, his heart still thundering in his chest. He was just marginally relaxing when a searing pain ripped through his side as a bullet tore into his flesh. He grunted, clenching his jaw to stifle any outcry that might alert the others. Adrenaline coursed through his veins, dulling the agony for now, but the wound was serious.

Sawyer's truck careened wildly, the tires kicking up plumes of dust as they raced away from the ambush. Viper pulled Sage closer, shielding her body with his own as bullets pinged off the truck's exterior.

"You hit?" shouted Sawyer over the roar of the engine, his eyes flickering to the rearview mirror.

Viper shook his head curtly, his grip on his rifle tightening. He couldn't afford to show weakness now when Sage's life depended on him. He scanned the darkness beyond the truck, searching for any sign of pursuit. The gunfire had ceased for now, but their attackers wouldn't give up so easily.

Sage shifted beside him, her eyes wide with fear and concern. "Viper, are you—"

"I'm fine," he cut her off brusquely. "Just stay down and keep your head covered."

She opened her mouth as if to protest but seemed to think better of it, ducking down obediently. Viper felt a pang of guilt for his harsh tone, but there was no time for gentleness. Not until they were somewhere secure.

The truck bounced violently as they left the ranch road, jostling its occupants. Viper gritted his teeth against the pain, his hand pressed tightly against the wound in a futile attempt to stem the bleeding. Warm stickiness soaked through his shirt, but he refused to look down, knowing the sight of his own blood might rattle his focus.

Instead, he focused on the task at hand, mentally reviewing the layout of the rendezvous point Cooper had chosen. An abandoned farmhouse several miles from the ranch, it would provide them with temporary shelter and a defensible position until they could regroup.

The truck slowed as they approached the dilapidated structure, its windows gaping like empty eye sockets in the moonlight. Viper tensed, his gaze sweeping the surrounding fields for any sign of an ambush.

"Clear," said Sawyer, bringing the truck to a halt beside the crumbling porch.

They piled out quickly, Viper supporting Sage as she clambered down from the truck bed. He wavered slightly on his feet, the blood loss starting to take its toll, but he locked his knees and straightened, refusing to show any outward signs of weakness.

"This way." Mike led them toward the house at a crouch.

Viper followed, his grip on Sage's arm perhaps a bit tighter than necessary. She shot him a concerned glance but said nothing as they entered the musty interior of the farmhouse.

Once inside, Viper allowed himself to sag against the wall, his breath coming in ragged gasps. Sawyer and Mike immediately began securing the premises, checking each room for threats or signs that their location had been compromised.

"Viper?" Sage's voice was laced with worry as she crouched beside him. "You're hurt, aren't you? Let me see."

He shook his head, but she had already noticed the dark stain spreading across his shirt. With surprising strength, she gripped the fabric and tore it open. He winced as she cried out at the sight of it, looking over her shoulder to Mike and Sawyer. "Can you guys help me get in bed?"

43

Chapter 6—Sage

SAGE WATCHED IN TENSE silence as Nina rushed into the room carrying a large medical kit, her face etched with worry. Mike followed close behind, his usual brooding demeanor replaced by a focused intensity. She turned her attention to Viper, who was lying motionless on the bed, his shirt soaked in blood from the gunshot wound.

"Get him on his back," said Mike in a low, commanding tone.

Viper groaned as they gently rolled him over, his face contorting in pain. Her heart clenched at the sight of his suffering. She moved closer, kneeling beside the bed and grasping his hand tightly.

"I'm here, Viper," she whispered, her voice trembling slightly. "You're going to be okay." This was all her fault, having brought this to him. "How did they find me?"

Mike swiftly cut away Viper's blood-soaked shirt, exposing the angry wound just below his ribcage. She inhaled sharply at the sight of the ragged hole in his flesh, her stomach churning.

"Gangs have a lot of money and high-tech toys," said Cooper.

"It wouldn't take them long to link you to Viper via his link to Rahim. Then they'd just have to do a little more digging and discover his friendship with us." Sawyer paced near the doorway.

"They'd probably have to break into some encrypted files, but if your gang is big enough—"

"Or has connections to a cartel," said Kinsey while breastfeeding her daughter discreetly. The baby was calm and slept like she'd experienced nothing unusual.

"Good point, my love." Sawyer nodded. "It wouldn't take them long to find you."

"Which is why we had tight security and a fallback plan." Cooper's jaw clenched. "Didn't expect quite so many. I'm thinking this dude must have cartel or mob connections."

Nina handed Mike a pair of surgical scissors, and he began carefully trimming away the torn skin and tissue surrounding the entry point.

Mike muttered, his brow furrowed in concentration. "No exit wound means the bullet's still inside."

Viper let out a guttural groan, his fingers tightening around Sage's hand. She leaned closer, brushing damp strands of hair from his forehead.

"Just breathe through it," she murmured. "I'm right here." She looked up at Cooper. "It seems plausible. The R-7 gang just exploded into my neighborhood a couple of years ago. Overnight, everyone had heard of them. That suggests they had some kind of powerful backing, right?"

Mike worked swiftly, cleaning and disinfecting the wound before retrieving a curved surgical probe from the kit. As he did so, he said, "It was probably the Gutierrez Cartel. They're moving into Texas and trying to shore up the meth connection since marijuana is likely to be legalized at some point. Even in Texas," he said with a wry grin.

Sage watched him work, her heart pounding, as he carefully inserted the instrument into the jagged hole, probing for the bullet. Viper's body tensed, his muscles rigid with agony. A low, guttural sound escaped his clenched jaw as Mike located the projectile and began the delicate process of extracting it.

"Almost there," said Mike, his voice strained with effort.

With a final twist of the probe, the bullet emerged, and Viper's body went slack with relief. She exhaled raggedly, her eyes stinging with unshed tears.

Nina quickly handed Mike a suture kit, and he set to work closing the wound with deft, practiced motions. Sage kept her gaze fixed on Viper's face, willing him to hold on and to stay strong.

As the final stitch was tied off, Mike applied a thick layer of gauze and tape to protect the wound. He then retrieved a syringe from the kit, filling it with clear liquid from two different vials. "Antibiotics and pain medication," he said, injecting the contents into Viper's arm. "He'll need rest to recover, but the wound was clean. No major damage."

A wave of relief washed over her, the tension in her body marginally dissipating. She leaned forward, pressing her forehead against Viper's, whispering words of gratitude and comfort.

Nina began cleaning up the medical supplies, her movements efficient yet gentle. Mike rose to his feet, his expression grim.

"We can't stay here long," he said, his voice low. "Once he's stable, we move out."

Sage nodded, her focus solely on the man lying before her. She would stay by his side to protect him, just as he had protected her. All that mattered right now was Viper's recovery. "I'm sorry," she whispered. "Sorry I brought this danger to you and your friends."

A hand on her shoulder made her look up. She was surprised to find Cooper was the one offering comfort. He struck her as aloof and stoic, except with his wife and son.

"Don't be sorry. Viper wouldn't have wanted you to face them alone. You wouldn't have stood a chance, and he doesn't need that haunting him. We have enough ghosts." He squeezed her shoulder lightly for a second before moving over to join Caleb, who was sitting on the couch and looking a little dazed.

As the adrenaline faded, exhaustion crept in, weighing heavily on Sage's body. She settled onto the bed beside Viper, cradling his hand in hers, determined to be there when he opened his eyes once more.

The room fell silent, save for the steady rhythm of Viper's breathing, a reassuring reminder that he yet lived. She allowed the sound to lull her into a state of calm, her eyelids growing heavy as the events of the day caught up with her. Her eyelids felt heavy as she rested beside Viper, the adrenaline from the earlier chaos slowly dissipating.

Guilt gnawed at her, a persistent ache in her chest. If not for her entanglement in this dangerous world, Viper would never have suffered such a grievous wound. The image of his blood-soaked shirt burned in her mind, a visceral reminder of the price he had paid for his loyalty.

Despite Cooper's reassurance, she couldn't lessen her guilt. "This is my fault," she whispered, her voice thick with remorse. "I never should have involved you, Viper. You could have..." The thought trailed off, too painful to voice aloud. She swallowed hard, blinking back the sting of unshed tears.

Viper stirred beside her, his eyelids fluttering open. His gaze found hers, and despite the lines of pain etched into his features, a faint smile tugged at the corners of his mouth. "Hey there, beautiful," he said, his voice rough.

Her breath caught in her throat at the endearment, her heart fluttering traitorously. "Viper, you..."

He lifted a hand, silencing her protest. "Don't even start, Sage. This?" He gestured vaguely at the bandages swathing his torso. "It's nothing compared to what we've been through before."

A wry chuckle escaped his lips, the sound both reassuring and unsettling. "Remember that time in Kandahar? When that RPG took out half our Humvee? Now, that was a close call."

"I wasn't with you there," she said softly, worried.

"I know. I'm not delirious. I was addressing the room." He winked at her before adding, "We thought we were goners for sure. His voice grew stronger with each word. "Rahim he never lost his cool. Pulled our asses out of that hellhole like it was just another day at the office."

A fond smile curved his lips, and her heart swelled with pride at her father's bravery. He'd never told her about that, but he hadn't been the kind to advertise his heroic deeds.

"That's the kind of man he was," said Viper, his gaze locking with hers. "And you, Sage? You're cut from the same cloth. Tough as nails, with a heart of pure steel." He reached out, his calloused fingers brushing a stray curl from her cheek. "I wouldn't have it any other way."

Her chest compressed at the tender gesture, a warmth blooming that had nothing to do with the lingering adrenaline. "Viper, I…" She trailed off, uncertain of how to express the tumult of emotions swirling within her.

He seemed to understand, his expression softening as he regarded her. "I know, Sage. Believe me, I know." Leaning closer, he pressed his forehead against hers, their breaths mingling in the scant space between them. "You think I'd go through all this trouble if I didn't care about you? If I didn't…"

His voice faltered, and she holding her breath, her heart pounding in her ears. "Viper?" she prompted, her voice barely above a whisper.

He exhaled slowly, his gaze smoldering with an intensity that sent a delicious shiver down her spine. "I think I could fall for you. Might have already done so. Pain meds or not, that's the truth of it."

A breathless laugh escaped her lips, equal parts disbelief and elation. "You're serious?"

Viper's answering grin was crooked, a hint of his usual roguish charm peeking through. "As a heart attack, darlin', but if you think I'm just loopy from the meds, feel free to tease me about it."

Sage felt a weight lift from her shoulders, the guilt and self-recrimination melting away in the face of his candor. Emboldened, she leaned closer, her lips brushing against his in a light caress.

"Maybe I am falling for you too, tough guy," she murmured, her words a heated whisper against his mouth. "What are we going to do about that?"

The searing kiss that followed was answer enough, but a cleared throat quickly interrupted them. She buried her face against his chest, having temporarily forgotten they had an audience in the open, one-room farmhouse.

A COUPLE OF HOURS LATER, the thunderous roar of gunfire shattered the eerie silence that had blanketed the farmhouse. Sage's head whipped around, her heart pounding violently as she registered the unmistakable sound of warfare erupting outside.

"Stay down." Sawyer's gruff command cut through the chaos as he burst through the door, his weapon drawn and ready.

Sage instinctively flattened herself against the floor beside Viper's still form, her body coiled with tension. He'd fallen back to sleep, and she worried it was more than restful since this wasn't waking him. Through the window, she caught glimpses of muzzle flashes illuminating the darkness as Sawyer's team engaged an unseen enemy.

"What's happening?" Her voice trembled despite her efforts to remain calm.

Sawyer's jaw was set in a grim line as he crouched beside her, scanning the room for potential threats. "Mitch's gang. They must have tracked us here."

She glanced at Viper and felt a surge of protective fury rise within her. "They won't get to him while I'm still breathing."

Sawyer's gaze met hers, a flicker of respect evident in his eyes. "Then you'd better grab a weapon. Knowing your old man, I assume you know how to use one. We're going to need all the firepower we can get."

Without hesitation, she reached for the pistol tucked into Viper's holster, which someone had hung over the bed during the process of stripping him from the waist up and removing the bullet. Her fingers closed around the cool metal, and she was prepared to use it.

"Show me how to use it," she demanded, her voice steady and unwavering.

The sound of gunfire continued to rage outside, punctuated by the occasional bullet penetrating the old farmhouse's walls. Sage could taste the acrid tang of smoke in the air.

"Stay low and keep your head down," said Sawyer as he moved toward the couch, where Kinsey and Nina had taken cover, using their bodies to shield their children. His body was poised for action. "We'll draw their fire and give all of you a chance to—"

His words were cut short by a thunderous crash as the front door burst open, splintering inward from the force of a well-aimed kick. Sage's heart leapt into her throat as a familiar figure stepped through the wreckage, his face twisted into a snarl of rage.

Mitch Ramos.

The gang leader's eyes swept over the room, narrowing as they settled on her beside Viper's unconscious form. A cruel sneer curled his lips as he raised his weapon, taking deliberate aim at her.

Time seemed to slow to a crawl as her world narrowed to a single, crystalline point of focus. Without conscious thought, she brought the pistol to bear, tightening her finger on the trigger with a ferocity born of pure, unadulterated instinct as soon as she had him in her crosshairs.

The deafening report of the gunshot echoed in her ears, the recoil jarring her entire body. She watched, transfixed, as Mitch's expression contorted in shock, his eyes widening in disbelief as a crimson blossom bloomed across his chest.

He staggered backward, his weapon clattering to the floor as he clutched futilely at the mortal wound. A gurgling sound escaped his lips, his gaze locking with Sage's for a single, eternal moment before he crumpled to the ground, unmoving.

Silence descended upon the farmhouse, the air thick with the acrid scent of gunpowder and death. Her hands trembled as she lowered the smoking pistol, her mind struggling to process what had just transpired.

Sawyer's voice cut through the haze, low and urgent. "Sage? You all right?"

She blinked, her gaze shifting to meet his concerned stare. "I...I killed him."

The words felt foreign on her tongue, as if spoken by someone else entirely. Yet, as she looked upon Mitch's lifeless form, she knew the truth of her statement with a bone-deep certainty.

Sawyer nodded slowly, his expression grave. "You did what you had to do to protect yourself."

Sage swallowed hard, her throat constricting with a maelstrom of emotions she couldn't begin to untangle. Regret, relief, fear, and a strange sense of vindication all warred within her, leaving her adrift in a sea of conflicting sensations.

One thing was clear—she had crossed a line from which there was no return. Her life was forever altered by a single, irrevocable act.

As the weight of her actions settled upon her shoulders, Sage felt the world tilt precariously beneath her feet. She wavered, her vision blurring at the edges, until strong arms encircled her, steadying her trembling form.

"Easy there, Sage," said Mike as he entered the farmhouse from the back door, his voice a grounding presence amidst the chaos. "You did well. You kept him safe and took care of yourself. The rest of them are scattering now."

Sage clung to those words like a lifeline, allowing them to anchor her in the present moment. She had done what was necessary. As she turned her gaze toward the man who had risked everything for her, she knew, without a shadow of a doubt, that she would do it all again in a heartbeat.

ALMOST AN HOUR LATER Sheriff Dawson strode into the farmhouse, flanked by two deputies with weapons drawn. He nodded briefly to Cooper before his weathered face set in a grim line as he surveyed the scene—Mitch's lifeless body, the splintered wreckage of the door, and Sage beside Viper, who was now awake but a little confused due to another dose of pain meds from Mike.

"What in God's name happened here?" demanded the sheriff. "I got the Missus' call," He nodded toward Nina, "But I thought sure I misheard. Gangs in our area?"

Before Sage could respond, Sawyer stepped forward, his hands raised in a placating gesture. "It's true. We had an...incident with some gang members, but it's over now."

Dawson's steely gaze swept over Sawyer, his brow furrowing. "You know I can't just take your word for it, son. I need the full story."

Sage drew a steadying breath. "It was me, Sheriff. I...I killed him." She pointed to Viper's gun, resecured in the holster. "With that weapon."

A heavy silence descended, broken only by the crackle of flames in the hearth. Dawson's eyes narrowed as they settled on Sage, taking in her disheveled appearances.

"You don't strike me as the cold-blooded killer type, miss," he said at length, his tone neutral. "Why don't you tell me what led to this?"

Sage swallowed hard, her throat constricting. Where to begin? How could she possibly convey the harrowing ordeal that had brought her to this point, the terror and desperation that had fueled her actions?

"It started a few days ago," she began, her voice low and measured. "I witnessed a gang murder in my neighborhood. The leader, Mitch Ramos, saw me and threatened my life if I talked."

She paused, gathering her thoughts, and Dawson nodded for her to continue.

"I knew I couldn't go to the police. Not with the kind of connections Mitch had. We now suspect he might have cartel connections too. Anway, I reached out to an old family friend, someone I knew could protect me."

Her gaze flickered to Viper, a pang of worry twisting her gut. He gave the sheriff a loopy smile and waved.

"Vance Conley used to serve with my father in the Army. When my dad passed, he asked Vance to look after me. He was the only one I could think to turn to in the moment." She managed a small smile for the room. "HE brought me to this amazing group of people, who stepped up to protect me."

"We were holed up here, trying to figure out our next move, when Mitch and his gang found us," said Cooper. "They opened fire without warning, and Viper was hit trying to shield Sage. We fought them off long enough to regroup at our fallback location, but the bastards turned up here too."

"They probably searched every building on our property," said Nina. "It was inevitable they'd find this old place."

Cooper nodded. "We'd planned to be gone by then, but Viper's situation made it impossible to leave."

Dawson's gaze shifted to the prone form of the injured man, his expression softening ever so slightly.

"Mitch burst in, and I had no choice. Mitch was going to kill me. Maybe all of us. So I grabbed Vance's gun and..." She trailed off, the memory of that fateful moment searing through her mind like a brand.

"Sounds like you did what you had to do to survive, kid," said Dawson, his voice gruff but laced with understanding. "Ain't nobody gonna fault you for that, least of all me."

She exhaled a shuddering breath. "Thank you, sir."

"We'll need to get statements from the rest of your crew," Dawson continued, gesturing to his deputies, "But from what I can see, this was a clear-cut case of self-defense. Ain't no jury in their right mind would convict you, Miss...?"

"Collins," she said, her voice steadier now. "Sage Collins."

Dawson nodded as if committing the name to memory. "Well, Miss Collins, it seems you've had yourself one hell of a rough patch, but you made it through, and that's what counts."

His gaze swept over the room once more, lingering on the fallen form of Mitch Ramos. "I'll have my boys take care of the clean-up here. You and your friends, though? Y'all best hightail it back to Cooper's place and lay low for a spell."

He leveled a pointed look at Sage, his eyes twinkling with a hint of mischief. "Though I gotta say, with that getup and that hair, you sure as shootin' don't look like the kinda gal who runs in their circles. Not sure you're gonna be able to pull off the laying-low."

"She can lay with me any day," said Viper, sounding wistful and drugged out of his mind.

The sheriff laughed. "Best have Doc Holdings take a look at him in case he needs the hospital."

Viper clutched her hand. "No hospital. Not leaving you."

"You won' have to if the doctor says you're fine," she said softly.

"You just take care of yourself, Miss Collins," said the sheriff with a look of paternal concern. "And listen to those boys at the ranch. They may be a rough-lookin' bunch, but they'll see you through whatever comes next."

Sage nodded, her gaze drifting to Viper. "I know they will, Sheriff. I'm counting on it."

THE JOURNEY BACK TO Cooper's ranch passed in a blur, the rumbling of the truck's engine and the occasional crackle of the radio fading into a distant hum. Sage sat huddled in the backseat, her gaze fixed on Viper's unconscious form beside her, his head cradled in her lap. He'd fallen back to sleep on the trip, but Mike had assured her that was a normal side effect of the meds.

Every so often, her fingers would stray to his brow, brushing away errant strands of hair or tracing the rugged contours of his face. She realized he'd lost his eye patch somewhere, but it didn't bother her. She imagined he wore it for others' comfort rather than his own, but his scarred face was beautiful to her. Proof of the kind of hardships he'd endured and overcome. Each shallow rise and fall of his chest was a reassuring reminder that he clung to life, refusing to surrender to the grievous wound that had felled him.

As the truck rumbled to a halt outside the ranch house, Sage was relieved.

The others sprang into action, a well-oiled machine fueled by years of camaraderie and shared experience. Sawyer and Mike flanked the doors, their weapons at the ready as they swept the area for potential threats. Only when the all-clear was given did Cooper emerge, his gaze sweeping over Sage and Viper with concern and grim determination.

"Get him inside," he said to Sawyer and Mike before looking at Sage. "Nina has already called the doctor, and she should be here shortly."

She cradled his head and shoulders while the other men carried him into the guest room. It wasn't long before an attractive doctor with dark skin and locs arrived. She went straight to the guest room and closed the door behind her—in Sage's face. She didn't seem to have noticed Sage was following her.

As she reached for the door handle, a gentle touch on her shoulder drew her from her reverie, and she turned to find Nina regarding her with a warm, reassuring smile.

"He's going to be all right, Sage," murmured the other woman, her voice laced with quiet confidence. "These men are fighters, through and through. A little thing like a bullet wound won't keep him down for long."

Sage managed a faint smile, her heart swelling with gratitude for the kindness and acceptance she had found within this unlikely circle.

"I know, but I can't help but worry, you know? After everything we've been through, the thought of losing him now..."

She trailed off, unable to give voice to the fear that gnawed at her heart. Nina seemed to understand, her expression softening as she gave Sage's shoulder a gentle squeeze.

"You care for him," she said, her tone matter-of-fact yet laced with a hint of knowing. "More than just a friend, I'd wager."

Sage flushed, the heat of her embarrassment a stark contrast to the chill that had settled in her bones. "I don't know how or when it happened," she confessed, her voice a hushed whisper. "But somewhere along the way, amidst all the chaos and danger, he became...everything to me."

Nina's smile widened, her eyes crinkling at the corners in a way that spoke of hard-won wisdom and a lifetime of experience.

"Love has a funny way of sneaking up on us when we least expect it," she said, her gaze drifting to the doorway where Cooper stood, his imposing frame a silent sentry. "One minute, you're just trying to survive, to make it through another day. The next, you find yourself willing to lay down your life for someone else without a second thought."

Sage followed her gaze, her breath catching as she watched the tender exchange between Nina and the gruff, battle-hardened man. In that fleeting moment, she saw a glimpse of the depth of emotion that bound them. It was a love she recognized, a mirror image of the feelings that had taken root within her heart, blossoming into something fierce and indomitable in the face of overwhelming odds.

"Don't fight it, Sage," she said, her voice laced with a wisdom that seemed to transcend her years. "Love is a rare and precious thing. When you find it, you hold onto it with everything you have and never let it go."

Sage felt a lump form in her throat, her eyes stinging with the threat of unbidden tears. She nodded mutely, her gaze shifting back to the door. She turned the knob and entered, quietly observing the doctor examining him.

When Dr. Holdings had finished, she turned to Sage. "You're his person?"

She nodded. "Forever and always."

A small smile slipped through the doctor's professional mask. "You'll be glad to know he's all right. He'll sleep for several hours after the meds Mike gave him. I don't necessarily approve an Army medic doing surgery in an old farmhouse, but he did well."

"Good. Should Vance be in the hospital?"

The doctor snorted. "Should? Definitely. Will he? He's refusing. I've met him a couple of times, and I know how stubborn he is. Unless he gets an infection, I think Mike can handle taking care of him. I'll be by daily to check on him."

"I didn't know doctors did house calls anymore."

Dr. Holdings smiled. "It's rural Texas. I've even assisted in a couple of calf deliveries when Dr. Johnson, the vet, was busy with other births. A patient's a patient," she said with a laugh, departing soon afterward.

Sage didn't walk her out. She couldn't bear to leave Viper, who seemed to be in a restful state of slumber. Instead, she stretched out beside him and fell asleep.

Chapter 7—Viper

OVER THE NEXT FEW DAYS, Viper and Sage spent a lot of time together as they recovered from their harrowing escape. Cooper's ranch provided a safe haven, but the threat of danger still lingered. He could see she was uneasy, since a good part of his gang remained intact, and she was concerned about possible cartel ties.

That morning, she woke beside him, stretching lazily. He leaned closer, kissing her lightly before saying, "Morning. Thought you might want to take a walk around the grounds before the day gets too hot."

Sage nodded. "That sounds nice. Give me a few minutes."

As Viper waited, he admire her curves. He would have already bedded her again, but she kept shutting him down, insisting he needed to recover. She wasn't wrong, but dammit, how was he supposed to focus on anything but her and her luscious body when she was so near?

She distracted him by standing up and facing him, now wearing hiking boots. "I'm ready."

"Me too," he muttered under his breath, trying to ignore his erection.

Soon, they were strolling along the dirt path that wound through Cooper's property. The early morning breeze carried the scent of wildflowers blooming nearby.

"This place is like a sanctuary," she said, breaking the comfortable silence. "It's hard to believe we were in such a dangerous situation not too long ago."

Viper nodded. "Cooper has that effect. He's been through a lot, but he always finds a way to create a sense of security, no matter the circumstances."

They continued their leisurely stroll, taking in the tranquil surroundings. Viper opened up to Sage about his past, sharing stories from his military days that he had never told anyone else. That set the pattern for the rest of the week.

AS THE DAYS PASSED, their bond deepened. They walked every morning, having conversations about everything and nothing. One morning, after he'd opened up to her about his recovery time first in Germany, and then back at the VA stateside, Sage stopped and looked at him, her eyes filled with empathy. "It must have been hard for you. All those experiences, and then coming back to a world that feels so different and half-blind."

"It changed everything, but maybe not entirely for the worse. Things are looking up." He winked at her with his good eye and put his arm around her waist as they continued their walk.

ANOTHER MORNING, THEY discussed the aftermath of Rahim's death. "What happened to Loretta? I'm surprised you haven't called her, or she's called you while you're here. She must be worried."

Sage snorted. "She's not worried, and she's not much of a mother. Never was, but when Dad died..." She trailed off, looking sad.

"What happened?"

She hesitated before speaking. "My mother took all of Dad's life insurance and benefits and remarried within weeks. She left me to fend for myself when she ran off to Florida with her new husband."

Viper's fists clenched at her words. "She did what? That's... I'm sorry you had to go through that alone."

"It's okay. I managed." She tried to smile, but it didn't reach her eyes.

He reached out, gently touching her arm. "You shouldn't have had to." He took a deep breath, his voice heavy with regret. "I need to apologize for letting you down after Rahim's death. I was in a bad place, recovering from my wounds, learning to navigate the world with just one eye, and battling PTSD. I wasn't fit to look after anyone, let alone myself. But knowing you were struggling while I was consumed with my own issues tears me apart."

She placed her hand over his, her touch warm and reassuring. "You were going through your own hell. I don't blame you for anything. We all cope in different ways, and you were fighting your own battles. I understand that now."

He looked into her eyes, searching for any hint of resentment but finding only understanding and compassion. "I wish I could have been there for you though. You deserved better."

She squeezed his hand gently. "You're here now, and that's what matters. We're both survivors, Viper. We've faced our demons, and now we have each other to lean on."

They walked in silence for a while, the connection between them growing stronger with every step.

THEY FOUND THEMSELVES gravitating toward each other more and more each day. Over the next several days, as Viper continued to recover from his bullet wound, they spent hours talking, reading, and even playing board games. Sage hated the monotony of Monopoly, but Viper noticed the way her brow wrinkled in concentration as she studied the game board and the way she bit her lip when contemplating her next move.

He was captivated by her every gesture and expression, feeling his admiration and affection deepen with each passing moment. It was during one of their quiet moments together that he realized the depth of his feelings for Sage. The age gap that had once seemed like an insurmountable obstacle now felt insignificant.

That morning, Viper gazed at Sage, his eye taking in her beauty as she read in the kitchen. The way the morning sunlight haloed her took his breath away. He had known her for years, but it was as if he was seeing her for the first time.

As she turned the page of her book, a surge of affection rolled over him. He wanted nothing more than to reach out and smooth the crease between her eyebrows with his thumb. "Sage?"

She looked up, her eyes meeting his, and he was struck by the depth of emotion he saw reflected in them. "Yes?"

He took a deep breath, fortifying himself for what he was about to say. "I need to tell you something." He jumped to his feet. "Let's go for a walk."

She blinked. "Another one?" At his nod, she closed her book, giving him her full attention. "Okay."

Soon, they were walking across the ranch for the second time that day. He was restless and struggling to say what he need to say until she stopped and turned to face him, putting a hand on his chest. "What is it?"

He shifted closer to her on the bed, his heart pounding. "These past couple of weeks have been...intense, to say the least, but through it all, you've been a constant strength and comfort for me." He reached out, taking her hand in his. Her skin was soft and warm against his calloused palm. "Sage, I...I've fallen in love with you."

Her eyes widened, and for a moment, she was silent. He held his breath, afraid he had overstepped and had ruined the precious bond they shared.

Then, a slow smile spread across Sage's face, and she squeezed his hand. "Viper, I...I feel the same way. I've tried to fight these feelings, but they're too strong. I love you too."

Relief washed over him, and he pulled her into his embrace, burying his face in her hair. She smelled like wildflowers and sunshine, and he never wanted to let her go. "Your father was my friend, and he might not have approved of this, but I don't care. You mean everything to me. I want to build a life with you, if you'll have me?"

She pulled back, her eyes shining with tears of joy. "Of course I'll have you. There's nothing I want more."

He cupped her face. "When we get back to the city, after Sheriff Dawson clears you to leave, I want you to move in with me. We'll make a home together, just the two of us."

She nodded, her lips curving into a radiant smile. "Yes, I'll move in with you. We'll start our new life together."

He leaned in, capturing her lips in a searing kiss filled with promise and the hope of a future where they would never be apart again.

Chapter 8—Sage

SAGE'S HEART RACED after Viper's words of love. She gazed into his striking blue eye, reading the sincerity there. Without a word, she took his calloused hand and led him toward the nearest barn on Cooper's property.

The scent of hay and leather from old saddles mounted to the wall surrounded them as they entered the dimly lit space. Sage's fingers trembled slightly as she undid the buttons of her blouse, letting it slide off her shoulders and pool at her feet. Viper watched her intently, his gaze roaming appreciatively over the curves highlighted by her lacy bra and tight jeans.

Stepping closer, he cupped her face tenderly before capturing her lips in a searing kiss. She melted into his embrace, tangling her fingers in his short hair as she returned the passionate caress. Their tongues danced together in a sensual rhythm.

Breaking the kiss, he trailed his lips along her jawline down to her neck. She tilted back her head with a soft sigh, reveling in the sensation of his stubble grazing her sensitive skin. His hands roamed down her sides to settle on her hips, pulling her flush against his cock straining against his jeans.

With deft motions, he unclasped her bra and pushed aside the lacy garment, baring her full breasts to his heated gaze. He palmed the soft mounds, brushing his thumbs over the taut peaks. She arched into his touch with a whimper of pleasure but paused, grasping his hair. "We shouldn't..."

He grunted. "I'm fine. Dr. Holdings said I could go back to regular activities, remember?"

"I'm just worried you'll be hurt again." She couldn't hide her fear at the memory of him almost dying.

He groaned. "Honey, if I don't get balls-deep in you real soon, I might die."

That made her giggle, and she surrendered, setting aside her fear that he wasn't ready for vigorous lovemaking yet.

Lowering himself to his knees, he pressed open-mouthed kisses along the valley between her breasts. His hands slid down to unfasten her jeans, tugging them over her hips and allowing them to fall in a puddle around her ankles. She stepped out of them, kicking off her shoes as well until she stood gloriously nude before him.

His eye darkened with desire. Grasping her hips, he guided her to lay back on the soft mound of hay covered by a thick horse blanket. Her skin tingled with anticipation as he settled between her parted thighs.

His mouth found her pussy, tongue flicking out to tease her slick folds. Sage gasped sharply, arching her back as waves of pleasure radiated through from her clit. Viper lapped at her with broad strokes, alternating with focused attention on her aching bud.

She writhed beneath his skilled ministrations, clutching at the hay. Soft mewls of ecstasy escaped her parted lips as the tension within her coiled tighter and tighter. With a final flick of his tongue, she shattered, crying out his name as her release washed over her in blissful pulses.

Panting heavily and still in the midst of bliss, she tugged up Viper for a ravenous kiss, tasting herself on his lips and tongue. Her hands made quick work of his belt and zipper, pushing his jeans and boxers down just enough to free his rigid cock. Wrapping her fingers around the velvety shaft, she stroked him firmly from root to tip, relishing the low groan that rumbled in his throat.

Breaking the kiss, she pushed lightly against his chest until he rolled onto his back on the blanket. Sage rose up on her knees and leaned over him, taking his cock into her mouth in one smooth motion until the tip nudged the back of her throat.

Viper hissed sharply through clenched teeth as her lips slid up and down his shaft. She lavished attention on the sensitive head before taking him deeply once more. His fingers threaded through her purple curls as she established a rhythmic bobbing, hollowing her cheeks to increase the suction.

All too soon, he gently pulled her off him with a regretful groan. She looked at him with heavy-lidded eyes, her lips feeling swollen and slick. In one fluid motion, he flipped her onto her back and settled between her thighs once more.

Positioning himself at her entrance, he locked eyes with her as he pushed forward in one smooth thrust, sheathing his cock fully inside her welcoming heat. Sage gasped at the delicious fullness, wrapping her legs around his waist to take him even deeper.

Viper set a languid pace, rolling his hips in a sensual grind that stoked the smoldering ember within her. She matched his rhythm, meeting his thrusts as their bodies moved together in perfect synchronicity.

Their harsh pants and soft moans mingled with the rustle of the hay as their lovemaking built to a fevered pitch. She raked her nails down the rippling muscles of his back as he drove into her with increasing urgency. Her release was building once more, the exquisite tension cresting higher with each stroke.

"Viper..." She whimpered, clinging to him as her climax crashed over her in shattering waves. He followed her over the edge with a hoarse shout, his release pulsing deep within her in hot spurts.

Spent, he collapsed atop her, burying his face against the curve of her neck as they caught their breath. She carded her fingers through his sweat-dampened hair, basking in the afterglow.

For long moments, they lay tangled together in sated silence, the only sounds their mingled breathing and the soft lowing of cattle in the distance. Sage was at peace, her fears and the dangers they faced momentarily forgotten in the refuge of his arms.

SAGE'S PHONE VIBRATED against her hip as she sat on the porch of Cooper's ranch, enjoying the warm Texas afternoon. She pulled it out, expecting a message from Viper about his trip into town for supplies. Instead, her blood ran cold as she saw a text from Chloe's phone number.

The screen displayed a photo of Chloe, bound and gagged, terror evident in her wide eyes. Below it was a message: *"Trade your life for hers. Come to Chicago alone or she dies. —Miguel"*

Her hands trembled as she stared at the image. She burst into the house, nearly colliding with Nina in the kitchen. "We have a problem," she said, thrusting the phone at Nina.

Nina's eyes widened as she took in the photo and message. "Oh, no. We need to tell the others right away."

Within minutes, the entire group had assembled in the living room. Sage paced anxiously as she explained the situation to Cooper, Mike, and the newly-returned Viper.

"We can't let you go," said Viper firmly. "It's clearly a trap."

Sage whirled to face him. "I can't let Chloe die because of me. She's innocent in all this."

"So are you, Sage." Cooper leaned forward, resting his elbows on his knees. "No one's saying we'll abandon your friend, but we need a plan that doesn't involve handing you over to those bastards."

Mike nodded. "Cooper's right. We've got resources. Let's use them."

"What resources?" asked Sage. "Miguel's in Chicago. We're in the middle of nowhere, Texas. How are we supposed to find where he's holding Chloe?"

Viper's eye narrowed thoughtfully. "Sage, tell us everything you remember about the gang's operations in Chicago. Any properties or hideouts you know of."

"It's not like they ever told me anything directly. I was just a waitress, but I heard stuff…" She closed her eyes, trying to recall details from overheard conversations at the club. "There was a warehouse they sometimes used…near the docks, I think. And Mitch mentioned an old factory building once."

Mike pulled out his phone. "I'm calling Clayton. If anyone can make quick connections between the gang and property they own, plus get us satellite images of those locations, it's him."

As Mike stepped away to make the call, Cooper turned to Sage. "Anything else you can remember? Any patterns to their movements or favorite spots?"

Sage shook her head. "Not really. They were pretty secretive about most of their operations."

Nina gently touched Sage's arm. "What about Chloe? Does she have any connection to specific locations in the city that Miguel might exploit?"

"Just the club. Chloe's an exotic dancer at Club Neon. It's where we both worked and where I first encountered Mitch and his crew. It's behind the club where I saw Mitch kill that guy."

Viper nodded. "Good thinking, Nina. It's a logical place for Miguel to set up shop, especially if he's trying to lure Sage back."

Mike returned, his expression grim but determined. "Clayton's on it. He's got people checking property records and digging into the gang members, and then he'll pull satellite imagery when he identifies possible targets. Should have something for us within the hour."

Cooper stood, his stance radiating authority. "All right, people. We've got an hour to formulate a plan. Let's make it count."

The group huddled around the kitchen table, pouring over maps of Chicago that Nina had printed from her computer. They discussed potential entry points, escape routes, and contingency plans for various scenarios.

Sage's mind raced as she listened to the others strategize. The guilt of putting Chloe in danger warred with her fear of facing Miguel and his crew again. Underneath it all, a fierce determination burned. She wouldn't let Chloe suffer because of her. And she sure as hell wasn't going to let Miguel win.

Mike's phone buzzed, and he quickly answered it. After a brief conversation, he hung up and addressed the group. "Clayton's got something. He's sending the images now. He confirmed Mitch Ramos owned a warehouse, and Miguel owns a rundown factory. Club Neon was a bust. The club is owned by someone not connected to the gang, as far as he could learn, and it seems unlikely they'd risk their venue and livelihood to set up a trap for Sage."

They crowded around Mike's laptop as the files downloaded. Satellite photos of a rundown factory appeared first. Thermal imaging detected no signs of life.

"I had no idea the government could see this much about us," said Sage, feeling uneasy.

"Yes, and it'll only get worse," said Viper with a scowl. "Let's use this to our advantage though."

She nodded, turning her attention to the warehouse that loaded. It was full of red dots.

"I can see why Clayton thought this was our best chance," said Mike.

Cooper nodded. "Seems like our best bet."

Sage studied the image, her heart racing. "So what's the plan? How do we get Chloe out of there?"

"We'll need to move fast," Mike said. "Element of surprise is crucial."

Cooper studied the rough map. "All right, here's what we're going to do..."

As Cooper outlined their strategy, Sage was frightened but also angry with Miguel and the gang. It was a risky plan, but it was their best shot at saving Chloe and putting an end to Miguel's threat once and for all.

"Any questions?" asked Cooper as he finished explaining everyone's roles.

The group shook their heads.

"Good," Cooper said. "We leave for Chicago as soon as Mike can get hold of Kat, and she agrees to help. Get ready."

As they dispersed to prepare, Viper pulled Sage aside. "Are you sure you're up for this?" he asked softly.

Sage met his gaze, her jaw set. "I got Chloe into this mess. I'm going to get her out."

Viper nodded, pride evident in his eye. "We'll do it together. I've got your back, always."

As he turned to his tasks, she stood for a moment, not sure what to do. Nina guided her to the kitchen with a motherly arm around her shoulders. "Don't you worry, honey. These men know what they're doing."

Sage managed a watery smile as Nina poured her a glass of iced tea. "I know...it's just, Chloe is the closest thing I have to a sister. If anything happens to her because of me..."

"Then we make sure nothing does. You're part of our family now, Sage, and we protect our own at all costs."

The conviction in her voice bolstered Sage's spirits. She took a fortifying sip of the sweet tea, determination replacing her earlier panic. "You're right. I can't lose my head. Chloe needs me strong right now."

Nina gave an approving nod before calling out, "Kinsey? Get in here, we need to have a little girl talk."

Moments later, the other woman joined them, an inquisitive look on her face. "What's up?"

"We're having a little support session of the sisterhood."

Sage blinked. "What's that?"

"The men have their brotherhood, but we have our own connection," said Kinsey, shifting Aoife to her other arm as she sat so she could accept a glass of tea. "We're not trained to save the day like they are, but we can soothe the soul and provide support."

She exhaled slowly. "Sometimes, that's just what a gal needs."

"Mmhmm. That, and some vodka," said Nina with a smirk as she got up and took a bottle out from under the sink. She poured a tipple in each of their teas, which further relaxed Sage. She almost had herself convinced she could do this by the time the sisterhood adjourned their meeting.

A SHORT TIME LATER, Sage watched tensely as Mike spoke into his phone, the conversation terse but purposeful. When he ended the call, he turned to face the assembled group.

"Kat has agreed to fly us into the city." His gaze flickered to Sage. "There's only room for a few of us though."

Sage straightened. "I'm going. Chloe was taken because of me. I have to be there to get her back safely."

Nina placed a gentle hand on the younger woman's arm. "Sugar, it could be extremely dangerous. Maybe it's best if you stay here where it's secure."

"No way." Sage shook her head adamantly. "Chloe is the closest thing I have to family. I won't abandon her to those monsters." She met Nina's concerned gaze steadily. "I can handle myself. You know that."

A heavy silence fell over the room before Cooper spoke up gruffly. "The woman's made up her mind. No use arguing." He pinned Sage with his one eye. "But you listen to Viper and Mike, you hear? They're in charge on this op."

"Yes, sir," she said, her chin lifting defiantly even as she acquiesced to his command.

Kinsey stepped forward, wrapping Sage in a fierce hug. "Be careful out there, okay? And get your friend to safety." She pulled back, eyes shining.

Sage returned the embrace tightly before turning to Nina. The other woman patted her shoulder. "You've got this, Sage. Your daddy raised one tough cookie." She smiled tremulously. "I'm sure he'd be so proud to see the warrior you've become."

Swallowing hard against the lump in her throat, Sage could only nod. She refused to let the tears prickling her eyes spill over. She had time to compose herself as they awaited Kat. When Mike wasn't busy talking to the others, she asked, "Who's Kat?"

He tensed for a moment, and she thought he might not answer. "My ex-wife. She's a pilot. Does small cargo and passenger runs with her own Jet."

It was clear he didn't want to talk about that, so she backed away, pacing for a couple of hours, pausing only when Viper stopped her for a moment to check on her. Then she'd pace again.

Finally, Mike got a text. "She's at the ranch's airfield." He stood up, looking reluctant. "I'll go pick her up. We might need a confab before we fly."

When he'd gone, Sage looked at Nina, who shrugged. Kinsey seemed as confused as she was, making it clear they didn't know much about the situation between Mike and Kat either. It must predate their relationships with Sawyer and Cooper.

Minutes later, Mike returned, followed by a woman who must be Kat. She was a tall, curvaceous woman with warm brown skin and an aura of quiet confidence. Her natural hair was cut in a stylish short afro, accentuating her striking features.

"Sorry I'm late," she said by way of greeting, her tone brisk but not unkind. "I had to file a flight plan."

Mike stepped forward, the tension between them almost a living force. "Thanks for doing this, Kat."

She waved a dismissive hand. "Like I'd leave you hanging when innocents are involved." Her gaze slid to Sage. "You must be the young lady I'm risking my tail for."

Sage lifted her chin, meeting the other woman's piercing stare head-on. "I'm Sage, and I appreciate you helping to get my friend back safely."

Kat arched one sculpted brow but said nothing more. Turning on her heel, she headed for the door. "I'm burning fuel just standing here. Let's get a move on."

As the others hurried to gather weapons and gear, Sage was alone with Viper for a brief moment. He cupped the back of her head, pulling her close until their foreheads touched.

"You don't have to do this," he said, his eye boring into hers intensely. "Say the word, and I'll go without you."

Sage shook her head minutely, reveling in his earthy, masculine scent surrounding her. "I can't. Chloe needs me." She brushed a fleeting kiss across his stubble-roughened jaw. "But I'll be careful, I promise. We'll get her back and come home in one piece."

His arm tightened around her waist, holding her flush against the hard jets of his body. For a suspended heartbeat, the world fell away until there was only the heat between them.

The spell broke as Mike's gruff tones rang out. "Let's move, people. We're burning daylight."

Sage pulled away reluctantly, offering Viper a tremulous smile before turning to follow the others outside after a quick parting with Nina and Kinsey. She hoped she'd see them again. They used a truck to accommodate them all, and she sat in the back with Viper. It reminded her of the last time they'd been together in the back of a truck, and she looked at his shoulder. "You okay for this?"

"Primed and ready," he said with a thumbs-up as they jostled across the ranch to reach the crude airstrip. Kat's small private jet was idling on the makeshift airstrip, the propellers kicking up dust in the dry Texas air.

As she climbed aboard behind Mike and Viper, the jet's engine roared to life, and they were airborne within minutes, soaring over the vast Texas plains toward the looming skyline of the city in the distance. Sage gripped the edge of her seat tightly. She was coming for Chloe, and God help anyone who stood in her way.

Chapter 9—Viper

VIPER CLENCHED HIS jaw as he surveyed the dingy warehouse where Miguel was holed up with his gang. The stench of stale beer and cigarette smoke assaulted his nostrils, but he refused to let it faze him. His eye scanned the area, noting the scattered debris and graffiti-covered walls. This was Miguel's territory, but not for much longer.

"We need to draw them out," he whispered. Cooper, the tactical mastermind, proposed using Sage as bait—a suggestion that made Viper's blood boil. Before he could protest, Sage stepped forward, her eyes filled with determination.

"I'll do it," she said, her full lips set in a firm line. "It's the only way."

Viper opened his mouth to argue, but the words died on his tongue when he saw the resolve in her gaze. Sage was her father's daughter—brave and selfless to a fault. Swallowing his objections, he gave a curt nod.

The plan was set in motion. Sage sauntered into the warehouse, her hips swaying hypnotically. Viper watched through the scope of his rifle, his finger caressing the trigger. At the first sign of trouble, he would unleash hell.

Miguel's men emerged like rats from their holes, their leering gazes fixed on Sage. Viper's grip tightened on his weapon as one of them reached out to touch her, only for Sage to deftly sidestep and deliver a swift kick to the man's groin.

That was enough. He wasn't going to leave her alone in there any longer. He lifted his fist to indicate they needed to move, and the men around him were on his six in seconds. Viper and the others burst through the doors, guns blazing. Chaos erupted as bullets ricocheted off metal surfaces. He moved with lethal precision, taking down targets with cold efficiency.

In the fray, he caught a glimpse of a woman he assumed must be Chloe, huddled in a corner. Her eyes were wide with terror, and she was crouched down on platform stilettos, trying to make herself a smaller target.

A movement in his peripheral vision made him whirl around, his rifle raised. Miguel stood there, a sadistic grin twisting his features as he held a knife to Sage's throat.

"Drop your weapons, or the bitch gets it."

Time seemed to slow as his gaze locked with Sage's. Her expression was one of calm acceptance, as if she had already made peace with her fate. A surge of rage unlike anything he'd ever experienced hit him.

With a roar, he charged forward, his rifle forgotten. Miguel's eyes widened in surprise, but before he could react, Viper was upon him. His fist connected with Miguel's jaw, sending the knife clattering to the ground.

They grappled, trading blows with savage intensity. He could taste the metallic tang of blood in his mouth, but he didn't care. All that mattered was ending the threat to Sage, no matter the cost.

Finally, Viper gained the upper hand, pinning Miguel to the floor with his forearm pressed against the man's windpipe. Miguel's eyes bulged, his face turning a sickly shade of purple.

"Viper?" Sage's voice cut through the haze of violence. "Don't kill him. He needs to face justice."

Viper hesitated, his muscles trembling with the effort of restraining himself. Miguel's life hung in the balance, and for a moment, he was tempted to snuff it out, but Sage's words overwhelmed his bloodlust.

With a grunt, he released the pressure on Miguel's throat, allowing the man to gasp for air. Sage rushed to his side, resting her hand on his arm in a gesture of support.

As the dust settled, he surveyed the aftermath of the battle. Bodies littered the floor, a grim reminder of the price they had paid for Chloe's freedom, but it had been worth it.

He was about to ask Mike to help him secure Miguel when the jerk reached for a holster on his ankle, previously hidden. Before he could fully draw the snub-nosed pistol, Viper shot him. Miguel fell, his arm going slack. The gun remained half-out of his holster, and Viper kicked it free while holding his Glock on the man, just to be safe.

When he nudged him with his foot, Miguel didn't move. He had a look of death that Viper recognized from his time in service. It left him feeling empty and regretful that the gangbanger had forced it to this point. He took no pleasure in killing him, but he'd do it again to protect Sage.

Cooper cleared his throat, the sound cutting through the tense silence that had fallen over the group. Viper's gaze swept over the carnage surrounding them—bodies littered the floor, a grim reminder of the violence they had unleashed. His knuckles were raw and his shirt stained with streaks of blood, both his own and that of his enemies.

"What about this mess?" Cooper's gruff voice broke Viper from his reverie. "We wanna stick around to take credit?"

A bitter chuckle escaped his lips as he shook his head slowly. "Hell, no. The less attention on us, the better." He looked at Chloe, still huddled in the corner, her arms wrapped tightly around herself. The poor girl had been through enough trauma. So had all of them.

Sage stepped forward, her purple curls bouncing with each purposeful stride. "Chloe?" Her voice was gentle, soothing. "It's over now. You're safe."

Chloe lifted her head, her eyes wide and haunted. For a moment, he thought she might bolt, but then she seemed to register Sage's words. With a trembling nod, she uncurled herself and rose to her feet.

"I...I want to go home," she whispered. "Please, I just want to go home."

Viper exchanged a glance with Cooper. Cooper gave an imperceptible nod, and Viper turned his attention back to Chloe. "Of course," he said, keeping his tone even and reassuring. "We'll get you out of here."

As they made their way out of the warehouse, he fell into step beside Sage, who had her arm around Chloe's waist. He could sense her eyes on him, studying him with concern and admiration.

"You're hurt," she murmured, her fingers ghosting over the gash on his bicep.

Viper waved her off dismissively. "It's nothing. Just a scratch. I don't even remember getting it." He eyed the wound, which was superficial. It didn't start to sting until he saw it. The amazing power of adrenaline.

Sage arched a perfectly sculpted brow, clearly unconvinced. "Let me take a look when we get back to the jet."

There was no point in arguing with her. Viper knew from experience that Sage could be as stubborn as her father when she set her mind to something. He gave a nod, and they continued in silence until they reached the vehicle they had "borrowed" from the airstrip, where Kat was waiting for them.

"I need to make sure Chloe gets home safely," said Sage.

"I'm coming with you."

"We'll wait here," said Cooper. "No sense stirring attention with a big parade. Watch your six."

"We will, but I think R-7's days are over," said Sage before he could answer.

They walked Chloe home. She seemed less shaken by the time she was in familiar surroundings and assured Sage she was fine. "I don't need a babysitter," she said, but not unkindly. "I'll rest, have a couple of drinks, and maybe even make it in for my shift. If I don't, Frankie and my landlord will kill me." She managed a wobbly smile. "Gotta pay the bills."

"Who's Frankie?" he asked when he and Sage were out of her apartment a few minutes later.

"The club manager. She's a real hardass. Scarier than any landlord," said Sage with a ghost of a smile.

They double-timed it back to the waiting vehicle, climbing into the SUV with the others. Cooper was driving, and he seemed driven to get out of the city. The reached the secluded airstrip outside the city, where Kat was waiting with her jet in under thirty minutes.

As soon as they were on board the Pilatus PC-12, Sage ushered Viper into the small bathroom, her touch gentle but insistent. He complied, shedding his shirt and allowing her to examine the wound on his arm.

Her fingers were deft and sure as she cleaned and dressed the gash, her touch sending tingles racing across his skin. Viper mesmerized by the way her brow furrowed in concentration, the way her full lips pursed ever so slightly.

"There," she said finally, securing the bandage in place. "That should hold until we get somewhere more secure."

Viper nodded, his throat suddenly dry. Without thinking, he reached out and tucked a stray curl behind her ear, his fingers lingering perhaps a moment too long.

Sage's breath caught, her eyes widening ever so slightly. For a heartbeat, the world seemed to narrow to just the two of them, the air crackling with an electric tension. The tension crackled between them, charged with unspoken desire. Time seemed to stand still, the world reduced to the confines of that tiny bathroom.

The spell shattered with the roar of the engines as Kat brought the small jet back to life. Sage jerked away, her cheeks flushed, her chest rising and falling with rapid breaths. Viper clenched his jaw, reining in the primal urge that had nearly overwhelmed him and led to them joining the Mile High Club while still on the ground.

They emerged from the bathroom to find the others strapping themselves in for takeoff. Cooper shot them a questioning glance, his brow furrowed, but remained silent. Viper settled into his seat, taut with pent-up tension.

The flight was smooth, allowing them all the needed time to decompress after the mission. He kept a close eye on Sage, but she seemed to be recovering well. As the jet touched down on the ranch's makeshift airstrip nearly four hours later, Viper allowed himself a moment to gather his composure before he followed the others off the jet and into the cool night air.

The ranch loomed before them and he felt a sense of homecoming wash over him as they approached the familiar structure. Cooper ushered them inside, his gruff demeanor softening as he greeted Nina and Caleb.

As the others dispersed, they went straight to the guest room they were sharing. He needed rest, but more than that, he needed to feel her skin against his and reassure himself they were both whole, alive, and well. She apparently needed that too, because she took his hand and walked eagerly at his side.

A FEW DAYS LATER, WHEN everything seemed to have calmed down, Viper felt like he could breathe again. They'd been closely watching the Chicago news, but they had no concerns. Police had decided it was a turf war with a rival gang, and the case was closed.

Just today, Sheriff Dawson had cleared Sage to leave town, so there was no reason they had to stay. She seemed a little despondent about that as he approached her that night. "Can we talk outside?"

Sage nodded, her gaze locked with his. "Lead the way."

Viper guided her through the ranch house, his footsteps echoing on the hardwood floors. They passed through a set of double doors and emerged onto a sprawling patio, the night sky stretching out above them like a velvet canopy studded with diamonds.

Sage inhaled deeply, savoring the crisp night air. "It's beautiful here. I don't think I'll ever get used to that—not that I'll be staying much longer." She sounded sad for a second.

He nodded. "It is. This place..." He trailed off, searching for the right words. "It's more than just a ranch. It's a place where we can be ourselves without fear or judgment. The most important people in my life gather here, including you. My life is here in many ways, but the most important person has a life somewhere else."

Sage turned to face him, her expression solemn. "What are you trying to say, Viper?"

He took a deep breath, steeling himself for what he was about to do. "Sage, you know how I feel about you. Hell, I think the whole damn world knows at this point." A wry smile tugged at his lips. "But what you don't know is how much you mean to me. How much your safety, your happiness, means to me."

Sage's eyes widened, her full lips parting in surprise. Before she could respond, he pressed on.

"I've been carrying this weight for too long, and it's time I let it go." He reached into his pocket and withdrew a small velvet box, his fingers trembling ever so slightly. "Sage Collins, you are the strongest, bravest, most incredible woman I've ever known. You've stood by my side through hell and back, and I can't imagine facing the future without you."

Sinking to one knee, he opened the box to reveal a stunning diamond ring. "Will you marry me? Will you be my partner, my equal, my everything, either here or in Chicago? I'll go where you go, but this place feels like home."

Sage's eyes glistened with unshed tears as she stared at the ring, her hand pressed against her lips. For a heartbeat, the world seemed to hold its breath, waiting for her answer.

Then she dropped to her knees before him, her face bright with joy. "Yes," she whispered, her voice thick with emotion. "Of course, I'll marry you and live with you here or in Chicago."

Relief washed over him as he slipped the ring onto her slender finger. He cupped her face in his hands, tracing the curve of her cheekbone with his thumb. "You've made me the happiest man alive."

She leaned into his touch, her eyes shining with love and adoration. "And you've given me a new family, a partner, and a lover. How could I say no to that?"

He chuckled, his heart swelling with love. "The brotherhood and the sisterhood come as part of the package deal, for sure."

Sage grinned, her infectious laughter filling the night air. "All the more reason to say yes." She leaned forward, brushing her lips against his in a light kiss that promised so much more. There was a lifetime before them to fulfill every promise and more.

Epilogue—Viper

THE WARM TEXAS SUN cast a golden glow over the porch as Viper stood there, his gaze sweeping across the tranquil ranch lands surrounding their new ranch house. A gentle breeze carried the scent of freshly cut grass and wildflowers, filling his senses with the essence of peace he had found in this place.

His fingers traced the raised scar tissue along his cheek, a permanent reminder of the harrowing blast that had nearly claimed his life years ago. In those dark moments, love and family had seemed like distant dreams, forever out of reach for a battle-hardened soldier like himself. Yet, here he stood, evidence of the transformative power of unexpected connections.

The creak of the screen door behind him drew his attention, and he turned to find Sage emerging onto the porch, her radiant smile outshining even the brilliance of the morning sun. In her delicate hands, she cradled two steaming mugs of coffee, the rich aroma wafting through the air.

"Thought you might need this," she said, offering him one.

Viper accepted it with a grateful nod as their fingers brushed in a fleeting caress that sent sparks of electricity coursing through his veins. He took a sip, savoring the robust flavor, before setting aside the mug and drawing Sage into his embrace.

Her soft form molded against his, a perfect fit, as if they were two pieces of a puzzle finally united. He breathed in the intoxicating scent of her skin and basked in the moment.

Sage leaned back, her dark eyes sparkling with love and mischief. Reaching into the pocket of her shorts, she produced a small plastic stick and pressed it into his palm.

He wrinkled his brow, studying the object for a moment before realization dawned. A positive pregnancy test. His heart swelled with a joy he had never known possible, and he pulled Sage close, capturing her lips in a searing kiss that conveyed every ounce of love and gratitude he felt.

"I love you," he said against her lips, his voice thick with emotion. "You've given me everything."

Sage's fingers traced the contours of his face, her touch gentle yet filled with reverence. "And you've given me a reason to live, to fight, and to embrace a future I once thought impossible."

His gaze drifted to the glittering diamond and matching wedding band on Sage's finger, a symbol of their eternal bond. The sun's rays danced across the facets, casting a kaleidoscope of colors that seemed to mirror the vibrant tapestry of their lives, woven together by threads of love.

As they stood entwined on the porch, the world around them seemed to fade into insignificance, leaving only the two of them, united in a love that had defied all odds, and in the distance, the soft whinnies of horses and the gentle lowing of cattle served as a melodic accompaniment to their newfound joy, a symphony of life and hope echoing across the vast expanse of the Texas plains.

Her fingers intertwined with his as they turned to gaze out at the rolling hills, their eyes filled with the promise of a future they had once thought impossible

"Shall we take a walk?" he asked.

"Yes, just like every morning." Her lips curving into a radiant smile. Together, they descended the porch steps, their boots crunching against the gravel path that wound its way through their ranch. As the sun climbed higher in the sky, Viper and Sage walked side by side, hand in hand, and savored all the happiness and possibilities in the present and the future.

About Mia

THANK YOU FOR READING! I hope you enjoyed reading this book as much as I loved writing it!

If so, you might be interested in my reader club, where you'll get notice of new releases, specials, and other great goodies (like FREE books and FREE Chapters of upcoming releases).

As a special thank you, **you'll immediately get my book The Boardroom Connection, for FREE when you sign up**. No strings, you can unsubscribe anytime, and I promise I won't blow up your inbox.

What do you think?

<u>YES—I'm in! I want to know the moment you drop a new release and get my FREE book!</u>[1]

No, that's all right. I get enough emails, and I'll keep up with your new releases another way.

Again, I hope you enjoyed this book. You can learn more about my newest releases here: https://bwwmlovestories.com/latest-releases/mia-latest/[2]

---

1.   https://dl.bookfunnel.com/g14g65dcmd

2.   https://l.facebook.com/l.php?u=https%3A%2F%2Fbwwmlovestories.com%2Flatest-releases%2Fmia-latest%2F%3Ffbclid%3DIwZXh0bgNhZW0CMTAAAR34HFLR7qBe4ZmBHns_e4d0XgNzeLpuTKitrQtc8gfqYam6Jwke4d05P5M_aem_AXZgxaooVqdkRI8v5k6ceTy7Gin_SGSOwZ0mohUpkMmzR-Suzibzrob5LkW28qL53CXma0uvn_jG_N2FBJWICaiR&h=AT0CMUeqAaRQCxB-vibJCLOB3BJo5qSFoE64VilifGretJ6ZtzkQOn3BhZ4e4cTX1Dpuw0RpYrElXkhsQlqHZNi1DZdWlWOBOS2jn6YcuV5YinE0EhazJOy56rM3zQC4ziRiIOHCHTe8ohj45g&__tn__=-

And if you get a chance to drop a review or rating, I'd really appreciate it.

Best,

Mia

UK-

R&c%5b0%5d=AT06pfvEYO5wdSYGkilnE_RlU_XJQ3YtaKVXM3kw2RVJU7AEHMWZr

Kbz4ZVZ5KpHSvCa7Rpb3D9k4_NQuxDrhwHZHAVAvzrcdwCUjfoVuAu6L2M3OoNNZ

9qa849xyadSBygYxrAoFCijWjBix80lUGrim2l7h4DWuGnd8vRM3D-hcJAbp-

sg41WLy5X32P7Q

About Mylia

IF YOU WOULD LIKE TO be the first to hear about new releases, please join my mailing list[1] and receive a free book. I love to hear from readers, so please feel free to email me at myliaashton@authorcooperative.com.

---

1. https://subscribeto.eo.page/myliaashton

Also by Mia Caldwell

The Brotherhood
Saved By The Master Sergeant
Sheltered By The Sergeant Major
Shielded By The Staff Sergeant

Standalone
Marooned With The Billionaire Doctor
Enemies To Expecting
Ennemis En Attente
Feinde zu Erwartende

Also by Mylia Ashton

The Brotherhood
Saved By The Master Sergeant
Sheltered By The Sergeant Major
Shielded By The Staff Sergeant

Standalone
Vegas Mistake
Marooned With The Billionaire Doctor
Enemies To Expecting
Cynthia And The Prince
Desperate Measures
Inferno